The Battle of Prophets and Wizards,

Book 1: The Nostradamus Code and Vampires

Amir Moazenzadeh

Title: The Nostradamus Code and Vampires
Book Series: The Battle of Prophets and Wizards
Author: Amir Moazenzadeh
Translator (from Persian): Ph.D M.R.Ghanoonparvar
Cover Designer: Hamid Skandarian
ISBN: 978-1-939123-50-3
Library Congress Control Number (LCCN): 2014942386
Publisher: Supreme Century, Reseda, CA, USA
Prepare for Publishing: Asan Nashr

"Century VII, Quatrain 43: The night will come, the night when an army of prophets clad in white, like chess figures, confronts an army of wizards clad in black, and the battle will begin for which they have been waiting for thousands of years; yet, a greater battle is underway."

Chapter 1

Suddenly a dazzling white light covered far and wide and spread swiftly into the atmosphere, a light so intense, as though stemming from a nuclear explosion. At that very moment, the sound of classical music resonated through the air, growing louder and louder with each moment, until finally the eyes of a muscular thirty-year-old man lying on a wooden bed began to open, with difficulty.

The man's muscles of steel were sunk so deeply into the mattress it seemed as though he had spent his entire life on this bed. The sound of music continued to resonate, and with great difficulty, struggling to open his eyes completely, he reached out his left hand, groping toward the sound, and managed to grab and turn off the alarm clock resting on the nightstand next to the bed. As his eyes began to open more and his dark surroundings were becoming increasingly visible to him, the composition of his face changed. The music had stopped, and the silence that filled the room made him even more bewildered. Suddenly becoming alert, he looked at the bedroom, stunned. Even though he had not risen from the bed and he felt a heaviness throughout his entire body, he tried to resist and block the unpleasant feeling that was overcoming him. He looked around emotionlessly, as though he had been hollowed out from within. Only that white dazzling light…that alone was the last thing he remembered.

When a person is incapable of recalling even his own name, how could he have a sense of his own identity? Such a person is engulfed in confusion, and fighting with all the strength that he can muster, he tries to remember something from this past to grab onto for support, like someone falling off a precipice, even if this support is a small crumbling rock that could not possibly withstand his weight! He hoped to find some answer to the questions suspended in his mind, questions that danced before is his eyes, making him even more confused. An old round oak table in the middle of the room; a small bookshelf on the wall to the right, burdened with the weight of dusty books; and a puffy olive-colored backpack with gray, black, and brown stains suggestive of the backpacks soldiers carry on battlefields, with the tip of a long fishing pole sticking out, which was placed next to a cabinet right under the window. These comprised all the furnishings in the room; but none of them was familiar to the man. Agitation filled his anxious eyes. He only remembered that dazzling white light, and nothing else. What calamity had actually befallen him? Had they totally erased his mind? Was he the sole survivor of a nuclear explosion? He sat in the middle of the wooden bed, as motionless as a statue. Perhaps he had surrendered to all the questions that had wrapped a rope around his mind, each of which pulled his mind in a different direction. No matter how desperately he tried to find an answer to these questions, it was in vain. Some time passed before he could decide to get out of the bed and look for a sign that could perhaps rid him of this confusion. Slowly he placed the heels of his feet, as heavy as lead, on the ground; but the black military boots he was wearing prevented him from feeling the hardness of the brown wooden floor. To maintain his balance, he placed his hands on the corner of the bed, which emitted loud squeaky sounds, for support and managed to stand up on his legs. Despite the fact that the heaviness of the boots tormented him, like chains and shackles, he advanced a few steps to the middle of the room, where the reflection of sunlight on a white object on the old wooden table drew his eyes toward it. A folded letter next to a ship ticket was on the table. Curious, he picked up the white piece of paper. Squinting, he tried to read the writing on it. The writing on the paper said: "Mr. George Jackson! I know that you do not remember anything and you do not know where you are, but you must leave this place as soon as possible, because your life is in danger. The ticket on the table is for a cruise ship that will set sail at 8:30 AM. Pick up the ticket and the green backpack that is leaning against the wall in the room as quickly as possible and leave the house. Outside the house, a few meters from the door, a red automobile will be waiting for you, which of course you can see from the window of the room. Get into the car, and the driver will take you to the pier. There you will board the ship; and you must go to the top deck and start fishing in order for Mr. Michael Faulkner to find you. He is a professor of genetics, and he will fully explain everything to you. Mr. Faulkner is a man of about sixty-five years of age.

We should not waste any more time. I wish you success."

Now his sense of confusion compounded with a sense of fear, which made the world of his unknowns even more immense; but at least he knew that his name was George Jackson, the only thing that connected him with the past and a question to which he had been unable to find an answer up to that moment. Knowing whom he was supposed to meet to learn more was another point that he could count on; but he paused for a moment, and the lines on his face froze. He wondered how he could trust a letter the writer of which he did not even know. How could he be certain that his name was "George Jackson"? He thought, perhaps he was an important person and some people wanted to take advantage of his amnesia. As he was immersed in these thoughts, another thought crossed his mind. What if his life actually was in danger? Suddenly, he remembered the appointed hour, 8:30. In fact, what time was it now? If what was written in the letter was true, and it was now past 8:30, then what was he supposed to do? He might never be able to meet with Mr. Faulkner! With the letter in his hand, he hurriedly put the ticket in his shirt pocket, walked to the small nightstand, and anxiously gazed at the clock. It was 7:16. He sighed with relief, his mind set at ease somewhat. Now he seemed to have enough time to get to the ship. But he also discovered something else. He now knew that the alarm on the clock had been set by the same person who had written

the letter, the same person who wanted to prevent him
from falling asleep. But who was that person? Why had
he not awakened him himself, rather than setting the
clock? He finally turned from the clock on the table,
walked to the window, and carefully looked through the
dusty windowpanes framed in white. He looked with
intense suspicion, as though he were looking for a
murderer. He could see the red automobile parked
across the street. Of course, the automobile was far
enough away that he could only see the silhouette of the
driver. Could the driver be the same person who wrote
the letter? This was another question that had crossed
his mind; but in order to find the answer, he would have
to leave the house. The environment outside the house,
however, was unfamiliar to him. Perhaps he should look
around inside the house some more before he got into
the automobile with that stranger. Time was vitally
precious to him, but he might be able to find some clues
that would give him more courage to make a decision.
He took a deep breath and, trying to get hold of himself
and control his anxiety; he also placed the letter in his
pocket, and then began the search. The deadly silence
that surrounded the house seemed to confirm that he was
alone there; but if someone else were there, perhaps it
would be better that he not learn about the presence of
Mr. Jackson. George first went to the small bookshelf,
perhaps because the dusty appearance of the books
revived a strange feeling in him, a supernatural
sensation. Before leaving the room and going to other
parts of the building, he wanted to make sure that he had

not missed any clues and that the books were the first things that had attracted his attention. Among the dusty books on the shelf, he could see a book with a partly torn cover, which made it impossible to read the title. An internal force, however, drew him to the book, a strange sense that made him pick it up and turn some of the pages. The smell of old paper brought back a strange sensation for him. As he turned the pages of the old book, his finger paused on page 217, and some sentences on that page seemed to become more and more magnified, to the point that he could not look away from them or see anything else. It seemed as if a magnifying glass had been placed over his eyes to enhance his vision in reading these sentences. In a calm whispering voice, he began to read:

"And God made His special angel powerful and taught him many things; but the time came when the treason of that angel was revealed. At that time, God took back the beauty of his face and transformed him into a dreadfully ugly, fiery goliath. All the white feathers that had covered his enormous wings burned; his wings changed into hideously huge bat-like wings; and black twisting horns began to extend from his head. The angel, who now resembled a monster, vowed to take revenge and then flew away, disappearing from view."

When he finished reading the last word, he was suddenly overcome with an intense headache, and for a moment, vague images passed through his mind, as though a high-speed video was moving back and forth before his eyes, so fast that he could not even distinguish the colors. The book fell from his hands, and shutting his eyes from the severity of the pain, he pressed his left hand on his forehead, to alleviate perhaps somewhat the intensity of the pain. After a few brief moments, his headache subsided; and a few seconds later, no sign remained of that horrible pain, a mysterious headache that seemed unnatural to him. He bent down slowly to pick up the book, but precisely before his fingers touched the book, he suddenly heard a horrible striking sound. Mr. Jackson turned his head toward the sound. The sound was coming from a narrow hallway that led with twists and turns to the entrance door. He stood up, and looking around with suspicion, he began to walk slowly toward the sound. The sound repeated once again, as though someone were knocking on the door to the building with a large doorknocker. Obviously, some person or persons intended to enter the house by force. As soon as Mr. Jackson left the room and entered the hallway, before his stunned eyes, the white wooden door of the building shattered with the third kick, and pieces of wood flew into the air. A person in black boots and pants and a bulletproof vest on which the word **"Police"** was visible had covered his face with a black mask, exactly like the members of a SWAT team; and with the exception of his blue eyes, no component of his face was visible. With his determined eyes, he stared for a moment at Mr. Jackson, who was standing next to the bedroom door, perhaps wanting to make certain that Mr.

Jackson was precisely the person he had been ordered to kill. He aimed the large gun he was holding with his black gloves at George, and the red laser light emitting from the gun shown on George's white clothes. The earsplitting sound of shots being fired could be heard.

Chapter 2

He took a drink of water, but he still felt the drops of cold sweat shimmering on his face with his whole being. The pronouncements made to him by his grandfather in his dream were so shocking that he had suddenly awakened. He was still panting. Could his writing be so dangerous? He could not wait any longer; he would have to complete his mission before dawn. He wore a tunic like that of a monk, a long brown robe that included a cowl that completely covered his face. He put a silvery chain around his neck with a cross hanging down. He lit a candle, and holding it in his hand, he set off. Once because of his beliefs, he had faced the Inquisition court; but God had had mercy on him, in that they had not burned him alive! He did not want something like this to happen to him again. His hand trembling, he shut the door of the house and entered the alleyway. He would have to carry out his mission clandestinely. The sound of his feet could be heard on the cobblestones of the alleyway. It was a night of a full moon. Since the time he had lost his grandfather to the plague, he had felt very distraught and had dreamt of his grandfather many times; but this dream was completely different from the other dreams. He considered his writing as inspired by some supernatural power that he had inherited, and for this reason, instead of practicing medicine, he was now spending his time on a cast iron bowl full of water to divine things that were impossible for others to see. His grandfather's words were still on his mind. In how many hundred years are such incidents supposed to occur? It was very hard to fathom. He had seen that strange symbol many times in the bowl of water. Everything was linked to that strange, odd symbol, the same symbol that he had used in his writings many times but the meaning of which he still did not comprehend. The air was getting colder. He suddenly stopped for moment. He paused briefly. He felt strange, as if someone were following him. He turned his head quickly and looked behind him, but he saw no one, nothing but a brown stray dog standing quietly and staring off in front of a stone wall. He had never seen a dog act like that. The dog was standing as though it had been turned to stone. But he could not waste his time on a dog. He had to start going. Thus, he focused his eyes ahead and continued on his way. He was now taking quicker steps, whispering to himself, "I must save the world!"

Chapter 3

As she was looking at her golden hair in the shining blade of the sword, she began to think about the past.

"No, that was not good at all; do it again! You need to increase the speed of your rotation much more; and when in a downward blow with the sword, hold your arm straight. Feel as though the sword is an extension of your arm, a part of your own being." The old man was saying this as he was shaving his short white stubble of a beard. He was wearing a white Japanese gown, similar to those of the samurai. Sitting under a tall tree, from behind his bushy eyebrows, he was fully monitoring the movements of the girl.

"But Master," Elena declared, "I think that learning this movement perfectly is beyond my ability. This was the 236th time, and I still cannot do it!"

The movement of the blade stopped for a moment on the old man's face. Then he frowned and responded: "I have taught fencing to more than two hundred swordsmen; but I have not taught any of them this technique, because they were not worthy of learning it. If I am teaching it to you, it is because I believe in your talent. But time is short; you must learn it before illness finishes me off, because I cannot come out of the grave to teach you. So, hush, and continue practicing!"

Elena took a deep breath, made a resolve, and firmly moved toward the wooden ladder. She would have to prepare herself for another leap.

Suddenly, upon hearing the sound of the door to the room, she came back to the present. The man who was standing behind the door of their room knocked on the door twice and said from where he was standing: "Pardon me, Madam! The driver would like to place your suitcases in the car."

The girl said: "No need; I'm not taking much luggage with me; it is only a four-day trip." She then glanced at the photograph of a middle-aged man in an astronaut's suit in a gallant pose. She sighed and sheathed her sword in the scabbard.

Chapter 4

With every shot, the wood chips from the destruction of the wall of the hallway scattered and floated in the air, as though a slow-motion picture were being transmitted by a professional movie camera. George had succeeded in throwing himself into the room. The sound of the collision of the heavy boots with the wooden floor of the hallway resonated in the air more loudly every moment, and the person who seemed to be a member of the SWAT team was getting closer to the bedroom. George stood up swiftly and locked the door with the key that was in the keyhole. Perhaps he should have taken the warning in the letter seriously from the very beginning and left the house. His heart was pounding fast and he was panting. The sounds of the footsteps in the hallway reminding him of approaching death were like a heavy sledgehammer striking his head every moment. Now he was convinced that he had no other choice but to follow the instructions in the letter. He opened the window as he heard the shots fired at the door of the room. Mr. Jackson looked at the street anxiously, and then, holding the backpack in his arms, he jumped out the window. The bushes and short grass growing behind the wall of the room embraced him like a soft mattress. The door to the room shattered, and the shadow of a lethal weapon appeared on the wall, coming closer to the window at every moment. Mr. Jackson focused his eyes on the car and ran toward it with all the energy he could muster. His feet did not feel heavy any more, and he could only hear the sound of his own panting mixed with the sound of his heartbeat. In the meantime, the tip of the weapon with the laser pierced through the window, and its red light began to chase after Mr. Jackson. But before it was able to fire successfully, George opened the car door and, holding his backpack in his arms, dove into the back seat. Just then, the driver, with headphones on his ears, turned his head and, with eyes open wide while removing his headphones, sized up Mr. Jackson as if some creature from outer space had dropped from the sky into his car! Most likely, the headphones with which he had been listening to music had prevented his hearing the shots, and he had been relaxing peacefully in the car seat. George, who was spread out on the back seat, raised his head a little, and shushing, he swallowed the saliva in his mouth and said, "Take off!" The driver, very confused by George's behavior, continued staring at him when suddenly the sound of a gunshot resonated in the air and the back window of the car shattered and came crashing down. The gunshot, the shattering of the car window, and the yelling of Mr. Jackson, "Hurry up, take off!" were three factors that led the driver to comprehend fully the circumstances. Then, nodding his head in agreement, he turned the key. The engine roared. He pressed his foot heavily on the gas pedal. Now the car was zigzagging in the street, speeding farther and farther away from the house at every moment.

Chapter 5

"I must save the world! This morning, my book will go to print; and before one word of the text is printed, I must remove those pages. I must not give reason to the publisher, because he might suspect me. No one must learn about this. Most likely, the publisher will also not notice that part of the text is missing. I am certain he has not read the text carefully, even once..." As these words were passing through his mind, he failed to notice the cold weather, or the hot candle wax that was dripping on his hand. For the first time in his entire life, he wanted to steal; and stealing those sheets of paper seemed to him a sacred duty, perhaps the most sacred thing he was capable of doing.

The sound of his footsteps could be heard. He had no more than 100 meters left to go. He prayed to God that no one would see him stealing. Everything would be destroyed if he were caught. After all, how could he explain to these people what was supposed to happen in about 500 years? But he maintained his concentration, because he was very close to the printing house. He checked around and behind him; no one was there. He thought to himself that it would be better to enter through the window in the back of the building. It would be shorter and much less likely for anyone to observe him.

There were a few small trees around the window, but he did not consider them an obstacle. He pushed against the window with both hands. The window squeaked and opened. His stomach fell momentarily. He looked behind him and checked the surroundings. No one was there. He sighed with relief. He was holding the candle in one hand and the frame of the window with the other; and he finally succeeded in pulling himself into the building slowly, without making a sound. The candlelight spread around, revealing the lead typesetting letters arranged in categories on old rusty shelves. These were the first printing machines invented by man. Usually, over the course of time, the erosion on the surface of the lead would result in the print of words not being crisp, and even sometimes the old lead letters needed to be replaced with new ones. At that time, however, this was the only available technology for printing books. He began searching. The air was saturated with the smell of paper, and the candlelight created a strange ambience. Even the small spiders that had spun webs in the corners and on the edges of the walls seemed to notice it. He examined the pieces of paper on the wooden table leaning against the wall several times, until finally he stopped searching. He moved the candlelight closer to the sheets of paper, carefully looking at them, and then rather quietly said, "That's it!" He picked up a few sheets, rolled them up, and concealed them under his cloak. After a few minutes, he left the building through the same window.

He felt that he had accomplished a great mission. He felt light, as if a heavy burden had been lifted from his shoulders. He headed back home; but he had not yet gone very far from the printing house when he noticed something. Everything was engulfed in dense darkness. Dark massive clouds rapidly filled the sky. The moonlight completely disappeared, and within a matter of seconds, everything sank into darkness. Even though he could feel the heat from the flame of the candle in his hand, the light of the candle had completely disappeared! The candle was lit, but its light was not visible! He did not know what incident was about to occur; he only felt that someone was approaching him. He could not see anything, and his entire being was overcome with anxiety. Before he decided to assume a defensive posture, however, the dark clouds moved aside, and moonlight once again made everything bright. He now could see the light of the candle in his hand. Intensely terrified, he mustered all his strength and began to run. He was running so fast that the light of the candle went out. He was not even looking behind him anymore. He ran without stopping up to the door of his house. He opened the door. Even though he was panting, he did not rest, even for a moment. He felt his heart beating intensely. Immediately, he lit the candle he was holding. Then, intending to burn the sheets of paper that he had stolen, he put his hand under his cloak, but most surprisingly, there was no sign of the sheets of paper. They had disappeared mysteriously.

Chapter 6

Silence filled the air in the car, and nothing was audible but the sound of the car engine changing with the shifting of gears. About two minutes had passed since that frightening incident and George's effort to get into the car. He had now sunk his entire body in the leather seat of the car and felt more secure and calm. It was that same feeling of elation a person has after a life-or-death experience, the same sense of euphoria that ensues with the rush of adrenaline throughout the body. This euphoria, however, could not hinder him from asking the questions that ran through his mind and were gradually frustrating him. He blamed the driver for this incident, the same driver who had not rushed to help George when he was in danger. So, without any prelude and before the driver could ask any questions, he raised his voice and in a demanding tone asked: "Who do you think I am? Why didn't you come to the building to rescue me? While I was struggling for my life, you were enjoying yourself listening music? And..."

Concentrating on the cars in front of him and maneuvering in the traffic, the driver glanced at him in the rearview mirror, interrupted the rattling questions of Mr. Jackson, and in a protesting tone said: "On the contrary, you are the one who should be answering my questions. Why did they shoot at my car? I almost got killed! I wish I had given up the money and had never come here!"

Surprised, George asked: "What are you talking about? In fact, why did you come here? Why were you waiting for me?"

The driver responded: "Look, sir! I have absolutely no idea who you are. Yesterday, a tall man with a white surgical mask covering his mouth and nose, who was coughing horribly, gave me a large sum of money and asked me to wait at this location until 7:00 AM for a man who is about 30 years old, and then take the man to the pier. Of course, he told me to be careful, and that I was not allowed to leave under any circumstances until you got into the car. But if I had known that this was going to be the situation, I would have given up the money and never come here. And now, I'm going to keep my promise and take you to the pier; and I hope we never meet again, because I have no stomach for trouble."

Then trying to pass the car in front of him, he pressed his lips together tightly in a sign of disgruntlement and shook his head back and forth in disbelief. Despite the fact that his mouth was shut, the vibrating growl of anger coming from his nose filled the air. Mr. Jackson, who had no answer, recoiled and said nothing further. Talking to the driver seemed futile, and the only thing that he wanted was to meet with Mr. Faulkner as soon as possible to find the answers to the questions that were driving him mad.

The red car continued to pass in between the other cars on the road, advancing toward the pier. Sunlight gleamed through the branches of the trees at the side of the road, reminding Mr. Jackson of the earlier dazzling white light. George rolled down the car window a little to get some fresh air on his head and face, perhaps hoping that the fresh air would drive away the troubling thoughts from his mind. Even though the wind did not tousle his short black hair, he squinted as the air caressed his face. Some time passed in this way until he could smell the salty air blowing on his face. Now they were very close to the pier, and Mr. Jackson was overwhelmed with anxiety.

About ten minutes later, George found himself in front of a large number of magnificent ships lined up at the pier, mesmerizing everyone. Without arguing with the driver or asking him any other questions, he had gotten out of the car a few minutes earlier, and now he was looking for the ship he was supposed to board among these ships that looked like cities floating on the water. The sun shone in the sky, and everything seemed calm. Finally, after some walking, the shiny white body of a beautiful ship rose from the water before his eyes, like an island, with its clear blue windows shining brilliantly in the sunshine. The stunning, modern design of this ship with five decks distinguished it from all the other ships, its name imprinted on its body in large blue letters, the same name that appeared on Mr. Jackson's ticket.

Chapter 7

She continued to hold the telephone in her hand; but apparently, it was useless. No one answered the phone. Once again, like before, a recorded voice asked her to leave a message. She glanced at her watch. She did not have much time. She hung up the telephone and said to herself: "I wish I hadn't lost her cell phone number. I should have called her house yesterday."

She thought for a while and finally made her decision. She was so excited that she could not wait any longer. She wanted to tell her in her own voice, before the news agencies reported the news. Then she began to dial again. Again, no one picked up the phone. Staring at a large poster of an airplane just as it was colliding with a tower, she left a telephone message. It took a few minutes for her to finish speaking. Finally, she hung up the phone, and still staring at the poster, she proudly whispered to herself, "This will never happen again."

Chapter 8

The ship calmly split the waves and advanced. Near the edge of the top deck, Mr. Jackson was sitting on a small chair, holding a fishing pole in his strong hands. Every once in a while, he looked around, anticipating the 65-year-old man. Suddenly his eyes stopped a little further, near the metal rails at the edge of the ship's deck. The long golden hair of a girl of twenty-seven years was waving in the mild breeze, and her long shapely legs forced her to lean toward the rails, such that only her right elbow resting on the shiny steel rails maintained her balance. Her posture, the attractive sexy curves of her body, her tall and shapely figure, the way she was leaning on the metal railing, and the way she had placed her right hand under her chin, gazing into the distance with her blue eyes ignoring everyone, all of this brought to mind only one thing: a beautiful, striking New York model! Nevertheless, her black military boots, her bikini of olive-colored, camouflage fabric like that of a soldier on a battlefield that she was wearing, and most importantly, the two katana samurai swords that were strapped to her back in the shape of an X with black leather, further distinguished her from the other passengers on the ship. Mr. Jackson was experiencing a strange sensation; he had not looked away from the girl when suddenly the fishing pole began to shake in his hands. He had no other choice but to pull the fish out of the water; but the fish was resisting with even more strength at every moment. It was obviously a large fish, whose strength increased several-fold as it struggled between life and death. Beads of sweat were appearing gradually on George's face, and his hands were turning red. As the struggle continued, suddenly with a rapid pull by the fish, George was propelled into the water, and the sound of his collision with the surface of the water attracted the attention of everyone on the deck. One of the passengers ran to the bridge to ask the Captain to stop. But a greater incident was about to occur. A massive, gigantic shadow was coming to the surface from the deep waters at an unbelievable speed, getting closer and closer to Mr. Jackson and causing turbulence in the water around him.

Mumbling to himself, Mr. Jackson questioned, "What in the world is this?" Now it became clear that the life-and-death struggle of the gigantic fish that had pulled George into the water was an attempt to escape this sea apparition. No more than a few seconds had passed when a large fin emerged from the water, splitting the sea like a sword, massively spraying into the air, and leaving behind on the surface of the ocean long stretched lines. The sea apparition was a huge white shark that had lost its prey and was now opting for Mr. Jackson as food. The shark's jaws were getting closer to George at every moment, when another shadow appeared. But this shadow, in contrast to the previous one, had nothing to do with the ocean. Rather, twirling around itself, it was moving above George's head, and for some moments blocked the sun that had been shining

on Mr. Jackson's face. The shark nearly reached Mr.
Jackson's arm with its open jaws; but before it could bite
off his arm, someone rapidly dove into the water
alongside the same shadow that had been flying above
Mr. Jackson's head. The dive was so quick and
thunderous, as if a seagull had dived into the water to
catch a fish. The samurai katana swords began to dance
in the water and cut two deep X-shaped wounds on the
shark's pectoral fin. The white shark quickly turned
around in the water and was now staring with its
frightening black eyes at the girl with the golden hair,
who a short distance from Mr. Jackson was putting her
dripping wet swords back into their scabbards. The
shark, highly provoked by the smell of its own blood,
turning and twisting, madly began to attack the girl.
Expecting this attack, she straightened her legs together,
arched her back, placed her arms like the powerful
wings of an eagle alongside her body, and pulled back
toward her feet. Her body moved like a wave, in a
butterfly stroke. She moved amazingly fast! She swam
and advanced with unbelievable speed, like a dolphin.
Drops of water scattered in the air from the backs of her
black boots, and at the end of every curved movement of
her body, she would pound the water with her feet
pressed together, and water would scatter in the air, as if
a spray emerging from the ends of her ankles. She
resembled a speedboat moving at tremendous speed.
She had begun a mad race with the white shark, a
swimming race in which, if she lost, she would be facing
the shark's jaws. The shark continued to chase her.

Everyone had rushed to the edge of the main deck and, so stunned at watching this competition, had totally forgotten Mr. Jackson. About one kilometer farther, a very large cargo ship was preparing to leave the pier and was raising its gigantic anchor from the water. In the meantime, the girl changed the direction in which she was swimming toward the cargo ship, advancing speedily in that direction. No one knew what she was thinking or how long she could continue this horrifying competition. Both the girl with the golden hair and the huge white shark were approaching the cargo ship very rapidly, and the distance between the shark's jaws and the girl's ankles was now less than two meters. With the raising of the anchor, massive volumes of water were pushed aside. Now about one meter remained before the large steel tip of the anchor emerged from the water, and the girl succeeded in nearly reaching the anchor. But before reaching the steel anchor, she slowed down for a moment, just long enough for the white shark to catch up with her. The shark's jaws opened wide, but before the sharp teeth could touch the girl's body, in the last jump of her butterfly stroke, she arched her back and with an astounding movement was able to pass safely under the steel anchor. At that moment, the sharp steel tip of the anchor entered the white shark's mouth, piercing through the upper part of its mouth before it had a chance to react. Blood gushed out, and the white shark, struggling with all its might to free itself, was suspended in the air, twisting and turning, and being pulled up by the anchor.

Chapter 9

The old man was hiding behind the stone wall. He had a very long white beard and long hair, and he was wearing a black cloak. A brown stray dog standing across from the stone wall continued to look inside the alleyway, and without moving or making a sound was watching the old man. It seemed to have sensed a strange power in the old man, and this caused the dog to stand there staring, statue-like. The old man waited for a few moments and then slowly stuck his head out from behind the stone wall. The man, who was holding a candle and dressed in a monk's tunic, was now moving more hurriedly, taking quicker steps. The old man came out from behind the wall and began to follow the man. He stroked his long white beard; he knew very well that tonight he would have to make use of his magic power.

Chapter 10

The woman and her husband were lying on the ground with their hands and feet bound. The wooden shelves in the room were filled with history and archaeology books; and of course, antique objects were also evident on the shelves.

A husky voice resonated in the air: "This is the last time I'm going to ask! What did you do with that infant? Where did you hide it?"

With tearful eyes, the woman looked at her husband's corpse and said: "How many times do I have to tell you that the infant was kidnapped? It was kidnapped twenty-seven years ago; believe me, I'm telling the truth!"

The husky voice that now flashed with anger resonated in the air: "Do you think that you have the power to annihilate God? It is you who will be annihilated." A sharp, lethal sword was raised in the air.

Chapter 11

As drops of water were dripping down on the main deck of the ship, the girl with the golden hair was sitting on a small chair, moving her fingers through her hair and squeezing out the remaining saltwater, when the sound of wet black boots were heard walking squeakily on the shiny wooden deck, and the long shadow stretching out on the deck approached the girl. Yes, this was Mr. Jackson, who was advancing politely and who finally stopped a few steps away, with saltwater dripping from his soaking wet clothes, a faint smile appearing on his face.

Quietly, he looked at the girl and said: "Well, I wanted to say that I am truly thankful to you. You risked your life for me, and I owe my life to you."

She smiled and uttered teasingly: "Now, did you learn how to fish? I wanted you to see that you could catch a fish even without a hook and a fishing pole. Did you ever think that it was possible to hunt a shark with a ship's anchor?"

Mr. Jackson laughed and replied: "Yes, you're absolutely right. But to swim at such a speed is miraculous!"

"If you believe in yourself, then miracles happen."

"How did you acquire such a skill?"

"You have to believe in yourself."

Mr. Jackson, who sensed that the girl was not interested in revealing her secret and wanted to evade answering the question with such answers, did not ask anything else in this connection, and only to show that he was a true gentleman, he offered, "How can I repay your kindness?"

She softly bit her index finger with her white teeth, and looking upward, she assumed a thoughtful posture and responded: "I'm very hungry. I swam a lot and have not yet had breakfast. How about inviting me to breakfast at the ship's restaurant?"

"Most certainly," Mr. Jackson said.

"So, let's first change out of our wet cloths," she suggested, "and I'll meet you in about fifteen minutes in the main restaurant of the ship."

Before the girl left the main deck, Mr. Jackson a little hurriedly said: "Oh, by the way, I still don't know your name."

"I'm Elena; and you are Mr. ...?"

Mr. Jackson paused for a moment and then replied quietly, "I'm George."

Chapter 12

There was a great deal of blood on the floor of the room. The young man pressed a small button with his finger, and a number and name appeared on the telephone screen. He knew this name, and this was the only clue he had. Sorrow and sadness prevented him from sleeping. He would have to start as soon as possible. He could not trust the police very much, because he suspected that a number of the members of The Organization might have infiltrated the police force. So, he decided to look for the murderer himself.

Chapter 13

Mr. Jackson appeared in the ship's passageway, the floor of which was carpeted with a very long red carpet, with wallpaper consisting of very striking gold designs. Now, instead of the white shirt with long rolled-up sleeves, he was wearing a black T-shirt that fully revealed his strong muscles of steel, a pair of blue jeans, and a pair of white sneakers that he had taken from his backpack. All this had transformed his appearance; but apparently, the new clothes were not important to him. In fact, when Elena asked his name, Mr. Jackson remembered something, the reason that he had come on this cruise ship. He would have to find Mr. Faulkner as soon as possible. For this reason, even before going to his cabin to change his clothes, he had asked for assistance from the ship's crew to find Mr. Faulkner, and had finally insisted so vehemently that they even checked the ship's manifest; but it became clear that no person by that name had boarded the ship. Now, neither did Mr. Jackson know anyone, nor did he have any hope of finding out his true identity. The only thing that remained for him to look forward to was having breakfast with the beautiful girl for whom he now felt a strange fondness, as though Elena had become part of his own being. Had he actually fallen in love with her? Even he did not know the answer. Moreover, Mr. Jackson was facing another problem. As he was searching his backpack, he realized that there was no money inside. His only possession was the backpack; and now he could not even pay for one meal. Nevertheless, the excitement of meeting with Elena, who was waiting in the restaurant for him, gave him great pleasure. Even if for one moment, he wanted to rid his mind of the thoughts that rushed through it. He took a deep breath, and in his white sneakers, he walked the passageway that led to a large glass door. Two ship's crewmembers in black suits and bowties pushed the glass door open with their white gloves, and softly and politely said, "Welcome!" Mr. Jackson entered the restaurant.

It was a very large rectangular room with glass walls, with the ocean in view from every side. A number of windows installed in the glass walls pulled the ocean breeze into the room. Numerous tables were placed equidistant from each other in scrupulous order, with white uniformly placed tablecloths and vases filled with flowers. Soft music was being played. As the high ceiling opened up, you could see the sky while dining. This is a description of the very luxurious restaurant on the top deck of this cruise ship. Mr. Jackson quickly surveyed the tables and walked toward table number 13. Two glasses of chilled orange juice, a piece of yellow Belgian cheese, two pieces of French bread, still hot, dispersing an enticing aroma in the air, some delicious carefully-sliced bacon, a small glass container of peanut butter, and a stick of butter that caught the eye with its golden color were all arranged on the table. The newspaper in the excited hands of Elena was so taut that it was about to rip. Her shiny blue eyes were following the lines of the newspaper. She was so engrossed in reading that she did not notice George at all, until he finally said, "I apologize for being late."

Elena lowered the newspaper from in front of her face; and with excitement in her eyes, she said: "George, you have no idea what strange incidents occurred last night, the least of which is the murder of a professor of genetics." Then pointing to the chair across from hers, she said: "Sit down and I'll tell you all about it." While pulling the chair out slowly to sit down, George noticed the suspicious looks of a young man who was leaning against his chair at table number 10, every once in a while jotting down something on a small piece of paper. Elena pushed the newspaper on the table toward George; and with her face beaming with excitement, she bent further, moving her finger in a zigzag fashion along the lines of the newspaper, and said: "The strange news that I was talking about is right here!" While George was squinting his eyes a little to see better, Elena began to explain the events with enthusiastic fervor:

"Last night the skulls of Beethoven, William Shakespeare, Nostradamus, Merce Cunningham, Blackbeard, and Michelangelo were stolen within a short period of time; and the interesting thing is that witnesses have said that a tall old man with a long white beard reaching his chest, who was wearing a black cloak and a tall cone-shaped hat that was the same color as his cloak, was the last person seen around that tombs of Nostradamus and Merce Cunningham before the skulls were stolen. Of course, some people have also seen a flying creature in the sky around that area that was carrying a large object on its back; but in that darkness, neither of them could be absolutely identified." Then, like a criminal investigator, she looked upward, assuming a thoughtful pose, and continued: "Of course, I think that the stealing of all six skulls had to be the work of that old man. But the question is, how could he have gone to multiple locations far from each other so quickly? And what did he want to do with the skulls that he stole? Another point is, how was he able to remove the skulls from the graves without making any noise that would draw the attention of others? How was he able to steal the skull of Blackbeard from the museum? What do you think, George?"

But she did not hear any answer from George. He seemed to be in a different world. All the while Elena was talking, he had been staring at the black headline of the newspaper: **"Genetics Professor Michael Faulkner Murdered in His Home."**

Chapter 14

A large eagle was sitting on his shoulder, moving its head back and forth. With his thin fingers, the old man struck one of the white clavichord keys and then one of the black ones. Both white and black had a specific meaning for him. It meant war, a great war that would soon break out. He would have to hurry; he had a lot to do, which he had to complete as soon as possible. He tied an old dirty rope to the metal ring attached to the wooden frame of the old piano, and he pulled the rope with his old wrinkled hands. The casters of the piano began to make a squeaky sound, and as the old man was pulling the aged piano behind him, he passed by the museum guards, who were lying on the ground unconscious.

Chapter 15

Elena, who did not hear any answer from George, shook his arm to bring him out of the thoughts and reflections in which he was immersed. Suddenly, the serious burn mark on George's arm that resembled a map became visible from beneath his short black sleeve. Elena asked, "What happened to your arm?"

At this point, George became conscious, and the first thing he said was, "Mr. Faulkner!"

Elena raised her eyebrows and asked in astonishment. "What do you mean? Did Mr. Faulkner burn your arm?"

George replied: "What are you talking about? What burn?"

Elena pushed his left sleeve all the way up and said, "This burn!"

Upon seeing the burn, George felt strange. Suddenly he had a severe headache; and for a moment, vague pictures passed through his mind. He pressed his fingers to his temple and closed his eyes.

In a concerned voice, Elena asked, "What is it? Don't you feel well?"

A moment later, his headache subsided, precisely like what had happened to him when he was reading the book. Mr. Jackson took a deep breath and said, "I'm fine, thanks."

"I apologize if my question made you upset," Elena said. "I didn't mean to at all."

George, who felt that Elena was the only person that he could trust and ask for help under these circumstances, took another deep breath, made up his mind, and finally explained: "No, that is not the reason at all. To tell you the truth, this morning, when I opened my eyes…," and thus he told Elena all that had happened to him in full detail up to that moment.

When George had finished speaking, immediately Elena began to fiddle with her wristwatch, and then holding the watch to her mouth, she said: "Hello Charlie! Get the helicopter ready! I will send you the ship's coordinates. A problem has come up, and I must return home as soon as possible. Please take off quickly. Thank you. Goodbye." Then, looking at George resolutely, she said, "We must prepare to leave."

"I don't understand what you mean," said Mr. Jackson, who had become quite confused. "Could you explain a little more?"

Elena looked around discreetly and then stared into George's eyes, and in a whisper that only they themselves could hear, she said: "Considering all that has happened, you should not remain on the ship any longer. Those who wanted to kill you might have learned about your appointment with Mr. Faulkner, and some of them might be on this ship. From here, we will go to my house, where you can stay for a while, until we come up with a solution. In the meantime, you might get your memory back and be able to remember everything."

Despite the fact that George still could not believe that Elena had taken all that he had told her at face value, he waited for few moments, and then nodded in agreement. The restaurant had become more crowded, and Elena and George left without even touching their fruit juice. How could they be sure that someone had not poisoned their breakfast, or even tampered with their glasses of orange juice? They first went to the bridge of the ship, in order for Elena to speak with the Captain about the helicopter that was to land on the landing pad, the one on the top deck in front of the main restaurant that was marked with a large black letter, H. After Elena finished speaking with the Captain, she and George gathered up their luggage, picked up their backpacks, and waited for the helicopter to arrive in Elena's cabin, which was more secure. George only hoped that they could board the helicopter safely before anything untoward happened. Attempting to preoccupy himself and keep himself from thinking negative thoughts, he turned on the television. The news network reporter holding a yellow microphone said: "Last night, Beethoven's piano was stolen from the museum building that you see behind me; but the museum officials…" Some minutes passed in this way until they gradually heard a sound from the sky. A red helicopter, the sound of the propellers of which resembled the flight of a gigantic insect, appeared in the sky. Upon hearing the sound, they climbed the metal staircase to the platform and were finally able to lean back in their seats inside the helicopter. With the vibration engulfing them, they left the platform, flying in the direction of Elena's house.

A tall man, his mouth and nose covered with a medical mask, in a husky voice with a formal, polite tone asked, "How are you, Madam?"

"Thanks, Charlie. I'm fine. Have you not yet recovered from your cold?"

"No, Madam. I have not yet completely recovered."

"I hope you get well soon," Elena offered.

Charlie coughed a couple of times and, attempting to subdue his third cough, said, "Thank you very much, Madam."

After this short conversation, all was silent for some minutes. George was looking out the curved window against which he was resting his head, as if looking for something he had lost. Perhaps he was looking for his lost memory in the water below them, or in the forest, the green panorama of which was visible in the distance, or in the sky above their heads. He did not know what he should actually do. How long could he stay in Elena's home? What if he never got back his memory? Even though now he felt safer, thinking of the future terrified him.

At this time, he felt Elena's warm hand on his shoulder. Elena brought her head close to his ear, and in her kind sweet voice said, "Don't worry! Everything will be alright."

George nodded in agreement and smiled.

Chapter 16

In a small room at the end of the theater building, he was hurriedly looking for a piece of white paper to write on, simultaneously repeating some words to himself. But his desk was very cluttered, and he did not have enough time to find a sheet of paper. For this reason, he decided to write the words on the blank corner of one of the pages of his play. He dipped the carefully cut tip of the eagle feather into an inkpot. First, he drew a strange symbol on the paper, and then he began to write the words. He seemed as though he were about to compose the most precious piece of poetry of his whole life. He wrote a few lines, when suddenly the quill stopped moving on the paper. He gave up writing, because he could not think of anything else to write. He tried hard for a few moments, thinking that perhaps he could finish the remainder, when suddenly a young man rushed into the room; and looking at him in surprise, he said: "William! What are you doing? Have you forgotten that we are supposed to perform your play before Queen Elizabeth? We do not have much time."

He turned around and looked at the young man. While he was enthusiastic to the depths of his being in his attempt to complete the poem, he had to prepare himself for the performance. He picked up his play and, without saying a word, left the room.

Chapter 17

The sound of the helicopter propellers continued until a large green enclosed area with tall trees appeared before them. At the far end of the area, a large palatial building with a stone facade that rose to the sky like a mountain with tall arched windows came into view, various parts of which resembled more a historical palace than a residential home.

"Well, we have finally arrived," Elena said.

George, who was staring out the helicopter windows, asked, "Is this house yours?"

"Actually, this is our ancestral home," Elena responded. "Don't you like it?"

"Oh, yes. It's really beautiful."

The helicopter was slowly approaching the ground. Finally, as the wind generated by the propellers made the grass of the lawn dance, it landed with a mild vibration. Perhaps now George could breathe easier. They tossed the backpacks over their shoulders, and hearing the sound of their footsteps on the green grass, they proudly walked to the magnificent building before them. After about 100 meters, they found themselves in front of a large wooden door with decorative brass cloves. It looked just like the door to an old castle. It seemed more like Elena had brought George to a museum. She opened the door, and they both entered this beautiful palace. As the door opened and they entered the palace, he felt as though he had entered another world. The air was so cool inside that he felt tranquil and comfortable enough to go to sleep right there. The entrance door to the palace opened to a large hall, a great room that was magnificent and seemed mysterious. It seemed as though all of history had happened in this hall, all at once. A high ceiling with classical paintings and distinctive plaster molding that framed the paintings, and its breathtaking beauty, resembling a church with gothic architecture, captured his soul. Luxurious chandeliers decorated with colorful cut crystal hung from the ceiling on golden chains. Shiny black and white marble arranged in a checkered pattern covered the floor, and a white marble fountain stood in the middle of the hall. The statue of an angel carved of white marble from whose mouth water was pouring out stood in the middle of the fountain, lit by a large skylight in the ceiling, which made the great room appear to be a sacred place, as though a divine light were shining down from the sky onto the statue.

"Angel, angel," the word repeated in George's mind over and over again. Yes, this angel and the light that shone on it made Mr. Jackson recall the book. Once again, the writing with the same large letters appeared very clearly before his eyes. He felt strange, as though he were being drawn into himself; and once again, that cursed headache returned. The same vague images passed before his eyes rapidly, and for a moment, he felt that he was lost in space and time. He pressed his fingers to his temples, and a few moments later, the headache was gone.

Worried, Elena asked, "Did you get another headache?"

"It's nothing. It went away by itself," George replied in a low voice.

"Did you remember anything?"

"No, like always, the same damned vague images," George responded.

Elena pointed to a corner of the great room a few meters away: "You'd better sit here for a while and rest."

Without saying a word, George followed Elena. Even though several brown leather sofas were arranged in a circle on the right side of the hall, Elena walked to a long wooden dining table that stretched half the width of the hall. The table seemed so old that it reminded him of the table that Jesus and his disciples were sitting at in the painting, "The Last Supper." Twenty wooden chairs lined either side of the table; and despite its age, the table was still solid.

At this time, a man of average height, who was bald on the top of this head and was wearing shiny shoes, arrived and in a formal tone said: "Hello,

Madam. Was your trip canceled? I thought that you would not be back for the next four days."

"Hello, Peter," Elena said. "A problem came up and I had to come back. By the way, this is George. From now on, George will be living here, and I would like you to treat him as you would treat me."

Peter was not happy to hear this. To him, George was an intruder. Peter did not like to see the Mistress with any man, because he believed that no man was good enough for the Mistress. But it went beyond this. Peter had special feelings for the Mistress, feelings that he never dared express. Nevertheless, concealing his ire beneath his forced smile, he said politely, "Certainly, Madam."

Then Elena turned to George: "George, in my absence, whatever you need, you can ask Peter. He is the butler, supervising all the servants." Then turning to Peter, Elena said: "By the way, Peter. Tell the chef to have the food ready earlier today, in an hour or so. George and I are very hungry. You can go now."

Peter made a short bow, and then clenching his fists, he left, taking long strides. With the sound of chairs being pulled back on the marble floor, Elena and George were seated at the table. George looked at the very expensive paintings hanging on the walls, and then asked a question that perhaps he should have asked much sooner, when they were on the ship or in the helicopter. He said: "Would you mind telling me about yourself? And..."

Elena smiled and said: "For a while, I was in the military, and finally I decided to resign. I wanted to have more free time to get to know myself and experience new things. Since my father died, it's been about two years that I have been living alone."

"Then, what is the story of the swords?" George asked.

"After I resigned from the military," Elena explained, "I went to Japan. I have always been interested in the Samurai culture. In Japan, I met a fencing master who agreed to train me. I was in training for about two years, when my teacher became very ill. But before he died, he gave me these two swords. I returned to the States after my teacher's death and have never been without these two swords, and..."

Minutes passed as they conversed. George and Elena were still talking when Peter came back, made a short bow, and said: "Pardon me, Madam! Lunch is ready. Shall I tell them to serve it?"

Elena said, "Yes, certainly."

Peter gestured to the servants, who then began to set the table; but before Peter left Elena and George to have their lunch, and as he took the first step to leave the hall, he remembered something: "By the way, Madam, I forgot to tell you that the telephone rang several times this morning. I think someone wanted to talk to you regarding an important matter; but because the door to your room was locked, I was unable to answer the phone."

Elena contemplated for a moment and then said, "Thank you very much, Peter, for telling me."

Peter responded, "You are most welcome, Madam." He then made another short bow to Elena, looked coldly at George, and as he whispered something to himself, his footsteps resonated in the great room and faded away.

Chapter 18

Some of the vegetables still remained on Elena's plate, and George was playing with the last green pea on his plate when Elena reached for the bottle of champagne. Looking at George, she asked, "Shall I pour you some?"

George took a deep breath and said, "No, thank you."

Elena drank a sip of champagne and then said: "I need to go upstairs. The telephone call to my office has preoccupied me. George, you can also come upstairs with me, and I can show you to your room."

George nodded in approval and said, "Hmm, okay." Then they walked across the shiny marble floor, and a few meters further, George found himself in front of a very wide, magnificent staircase made of white marble, with railings of the same stone embracing them on both sides, which continued to the top of the staircase. As George was climbing the stairs, for a few moments, he had a peculiar feeling. The short marble columns of the railing seemed to be standing in a position of respect for him.

Elena's office was on the right side of the staircase. They first went there. It was a beautiful room with large wooden shelves from floor to ceiling that covered the wall to the left; and, with the exception of a few picture frames, the shelves were packed with thick books on various topics. All sorts of medals that had been presented to Elena by the military also caught his eye in large glass display cases on the wall to the right. The remaining spaces on the walls were covered with space shuttle pictures. In short, it was a crowded room. Elena reached for the yellow telephone on her desk and pressed its red button to listen to the messages:

"Hello Elena. I tried several times to get hold of you, because I wanted you to be the first person to learn about this. I cannot tell you how excited I am. I really wanted to speak to you in person about this, but I have a flight in a few more hours and will travel thousands of miles to talk about this issue at a conference, where reporters are already competing to report on it. When it is presented at the conference, I am certain that it will result in a lot of controversy. Perhaps many will disagree with what I say, and say that I have made all this up; but I can prove what I am going to say. Of course, I am certain that the stealing of the skull of Nostradamus is not unrelated to this issue. You have probably heard about it. It has become a hot topic. Well, I won't take any more of your time. Let me get to the main reason why I called. Elena, to tell you the truth, I have made a great discovery. I am sure that you remember the book of the 1,000 prophecies of Nostradamus. I mean, Chapter 7 of the book, Century VII, the same chapter that instead of 100 prophecies, or quatrains, only has forty-two prophecies; and no copy or manuscript of the final fifty-eight prophecies is available. Many thought that for some reason, the publisher had decided not to publish these prophecies; but I was able to figure out what had happened to these fifty-eight prophecies. The night before the day on which the prophecies were supposed to be printed, a person entered the printing house and stole these fifty-eight prophecies, or quatrains. I bet you will never guess who that person was. The person would did this was Nostradamus himself! He stole his own prophecies in order to prevent them from being published. I assume that you are quite shocked to hear all of this. Of course, I will be back in three days, and we will talk about this in detail when I see you. I only wanted you to be the first to learn about this. So, until I come back, prepare yourself for a real adventure. Bye for now." Then they could hear a long beep.

Elena continued to stare at the telephone, when George stepped forward and said: "Your archaeologist friend was very excited! So that's why you were looking at that newspaper with such excitement!"

The telephone message made George feel that Elena was hiding something from him. But Elena sighed and said: "I am not an archaeologist or a historian; but Mrs. Hopkins is a history professor. She is the same lady who left the message on the telephone." She then pointed to a silver picture frame in the middle of the wooden shelves that contained a picture of Elena, who had her arms around the neck of a middle-aged woman, both of whom were smiling. This picture frame brought back many memories for her. These memories, bringing to mind her strong feeling of attachment to her mother, stirred Elena's heart and took her to faraway places. It was as though the sweetness of the tranquility and the sense of childhood security that she had experienced at the side of her mother many years ago mingled with the anguish stemming from her death. With sadness in her eyes, Elena continued: "That woman is my mother. On September 11, she was in one of the two airplanes that collided with the Twin Towers. After that incident, I participated in meetings arranged for the survivors of those killed in that incident. There, I met Mrs. Hopkins. She had also lost her daughter in that incident. Gradually, the relationship between Mrs. Hopkins and me became deeper, much like the relationship between a mother and daughter. To make a long story short, I went to Mrs. Hopkins' house for tea one afternoon and she talked about something that was new to me. She said that the September 11 incident had been previously predicted by Nostradamus; and she read some of these prophecies for me. These prophecies mention certain points, such as, 'At forty-five degrees the sky will burn' and 'a fire from the center of the earth shall shake the towers of the new city.' Then she told me about the decision she had made. She had decided to study all the prophecies of Nostradamus, hoping to learn about future events and in this way be able to save the lives of innocent people. She had already made up her mind and wanted to spend all of her time on this work. I also agreed that whenever I had the time I would help her with this work."

In order to change the mood and not cause further annoyance for Elena, very energetically, George remarked: "Well, for now, let us forget about Nostradamus. After all, in three days, when Mrs. Hopkins returns from her trip, she will tell us all about it. By the way, don't you want to show me my room?"

Trying to pull herself out of the memories of the past, Elena said: "Certainly... Of course, we have very important work to do today."

"Very important work?" George asked.

"Yes, very important work," Elena explained. "Tonight we have to go to Professor Michael Faulkner's house. We might be able to find some important clues."

Chapter 19

It was a beautiful room with two large windows that opened toward the green yard of the house. A comfortable bed with white sheets, a desk with a reading lamp, two bookshelves full of thick books, a full-length mirror on the wall to the right, a vanity table with a mirror in a beautifully carved wooden frame, and a wardrobe cabinet placed next to the table comprised the main furnishings of the room. The cozy, pleasant ambience of the room was quite feminine.

Elena asked, "Well, what do you think?"

George looked around the room and said, "It's great!"

"This was my mother's room," Elena explained. "When she wanted to be by herself, she came to this room."

Opening the door of the wardrobe cabinet with curiosity, George said: "It's obvious that your mother had very good taste, in my opinion..." The poster that was on the inside of the door of the cabinet stopped George from finishing what he was going to say. He scrutinized the photograph for a few seconds and then asked, "Is that that you, Elena?"

"Oh my God, what is this poster doing here?" Elena said, surprised. "This picture was taken of me when I was only fifteen years old. Actually, the company in which I worked as a supermodel gave me this poster as a gift. This was the first picture taken of me as a model."

"Oh, it's fantastic! Are you saying that you're also a supermodel?"

"Actually, I *was* a supermodel," Elena replied, "but I'm not now. I worked for that company for only two years. When my mother was killed, I was about seventeen. My life changed after the death of my mother. Everything changed. Why do you think I joined the military? Because I wanted to avenge my mother's murder; that's all."

"May I ask why you resigned and left the military?" George inquired.

Elena paused for a moment, and then tried to change the subject: "By the way, what time is it now? I totally forgot that we don't have much time. We need to find Mr. Faulkner's address as soon as possible."

Chapter 20

While George was finishing his orange juice, sipping it through a straw and mentally preparing himself for the nocturnal adventure ahead, Elena immersed herself in the laptop that was on her lap. Everything was quiet until Elena burst out, "I finally found it!" She then turned her laptop around, held the screen toward George, and as George walked toward her, sipping his orange juice through the straw from the glass in his hand, Elena's eyes sparkled, and she said: "I found the address to his house. Fortunately, it's not very far from here. It's only about an hour's drive. Now, finish your orange juice and we will get ready for the adventure."

Chapter 21

Two flashlights, a magnifying glass, a few meters of thick rope, and such comprised the equipment Elena was putting in her backpack. Of course, the two samurai swords, which were her permanent companions, were on her back. Elena would not go anywhere without them, because at any moment the possibility existed that there would be hand-to-hand combat between her and an unknown force.

George looked at her and said: "Did you forget to take your gun with you?"

Elena stood motionless for a moment, gulped, and wondered whether or not George had figured out what was going on. She waited for a moment, and then, to make sure, she asked, "What gun are you talking about?"

"You must be joking!" George replied. "Weren't you in the military? I thought that all soldiers in the military had to have their own guns."

Elena exhaled and absentmindedly explained: "After that incident, I decided not to use firearms any longer."

"What incident?" George queried.

"Nothing," Elena said. "I mean, leaving the military was a great incident. But, don't worry! My swords are very sharp; no one can harm you."

Finally, George and Elena entered a dark garage that was a few steps below the ground floor of the building, with an incline of about thirty degrees, which led to a green iron door. Elena flipped a switch and the light shone on an orange Ferrari that sparkled like a jewel, an automobile worth several million dollars! George, who was totally surprised, said, "This is fantastic!"

Elena smiled and tossed her backpack on the back seat. As they both got in the car, the iron door began to rise. Elena put her hands on the steering wheel and pressed the gas pedal. The engine roared. The headlights of the car shone like the eyes of a leopard. The car took off and from the incline bounded onto the street, speeding forward in a zigzag fashion.

The car was heading to the address of Mr. Faulkner's house, and its headlights continued to shine like the eyes of a leopard. The moonlight lit up everything; but it was not as bright as the previous night, which had been a full moon. After some distance, the automobile turned onto a wide road. Elena was used to driving fast, and now the road on which they were traveling gave her the opportunity. Now she had the chance to display her driving skills. Just like a Formula 1 racecar driver, she shifted gears, turned the steering wheel this way and that, and maneuvered, traveling at an astounding speed through the twists and turns of the road. Skillfully driving through another turn, from the corner of her eye, she looked with satisfaction at George, who was transfixed in his seat beside her and was digging himself into the seat with immense fear, and in a voice that resonated with mischief, she said: "Are you enjoying the ride? If I had known that not even the safety belt would make you feel safe, I would have arranged for a baby car seat in the back!"

Staring ahead with eyes wide open, George said in a trembling voice: "I...I...I'm quite comfortable. In fact, I love speed."

Elena smiled at George, a smile that clearly showed her mischievous demeanor, and then turning the steering wheel quickly, she went through another turn. The road was not crowded, and only once every few minutes would the yellowish light of the cars traveling in the opposite direction shine briefly on the faces of Elena and George as they passed. Some minutes went by in this way, until finally Elena slowed down. They were now continuing their way on a wide street on which nothing could be heard but the sound of the automobile tires on the asphalt. They were driving slowly. Elena was looking to the right and left very carefully until finally she stopped the car. Staring at an A-framed house a few meters away, Elena whispered to herself, "Number 63." She turned off the ignition. She looked at George and said, "There it is!"

George cautiously took a look around and slowly got out of the car. They picked up the flashlights, climbed the four steps that led to the entrance of the building, and passed under the yellow plastic strips placed in front of the door to the house to prevent entry. They turned the metal doorknob of the white wooden door. They heard the door squeak and open. Elena turned on her flashlight and aimed its circular light inside the dark building. The light shone on the face of the portrait of a woman in a gold frame on the wall at the end of the hall. Everything was shrouded in terrifying silence, as though they had entered a graveyard.

Once George had also entered the building, Elena shut the door. The faces of Elena and George were like shadows and could only be distinguished by the faint reflections from the flashlights. Elena said quietly: "Let's have a division of labor to get results faster. You search the rooms on the left, and I'll search the rooms on the right. If you find any evidence or clue, let me know."

George nodded and said: "Alright; that's a very good idea. That is what we will do."

Professor Faulkner's residence looked like a ghost's house, the kind you would find in a horror movie. George was not feeling good about being there at all. The thoughts that rushed to his mind made him shiver. What if in the meantime some armed people were to come to the house and the same thing that happened to him previously were to happen again? Could Elena's swords protect him from bullets? These and other such thoughts made his heart beat faster; nevertheless, he quietly went in the direction of the room that was closest to him. He tried not to think about someone with a gun equipped with lasers hiding behind the wall of the room, waiting for him. He advanced a little further. He could clearly hear the sound of his own footsteps on the wooden floor, and as he was swallowing, drops of sweat were dripping down his forehead. He reached the threshold of the room and shined the flashlight inside the room. This time, the circle of light fell on a wardrobe cabinet against the wall. George advanced slowly to the middle of the room. He still did not know what exactly he was supposed to look for; but he decided to start his search from that same cabinet. He put his hand on the handle of the cabinet and pulled it towards himself, when suddenly he felt a heavy hand on his left shoulder.

Chapter 22

The giant machine continued to excavate and advance. The noise everywhere was overwhelming. A middle-aged man in a safety helmet who was carefully monitoring everything asked the young man standing next to him: "Do you think the tunnel is wide enough for the shuttle to pass through?"

The young man said: "Yes, Sir! We have made all the calculations precisely. You can be certain that there will be no problem."

The middle-aged man, running his fingers through his salt-and-pepper hair, was thinking: "It couldn't be better than this. If everything advances at this speed, I will finally get my wish. We have to steal it from the museum as soon as we can. A lot of work has to be done on it."

But before a smile of satisfaction could appear on his face, he felt a severe pain in his abdomen. The pain was so severe that it made him buckle.

The young man anxiously asked, "Sir, are you okay?"

Squeezing his eyes shut, he responded: "I can't take the pain of this damned illness any longer. My only wish is to complete this flight before I die."

Chapter 23

George quickly turned his head, and seeing Elena's face, he sighed with relief.

"Quick, come with me!" Elena said. "I found the place where Professor Faulkner was killed."

Hurriedly, they both went to a room on the other side of the hall. They entered Mr. Faulkner's office. Elena pointed the flashlight at the floor and said: "Can you see this large dark stain? It's dried blood. I'm certain that they killed Mr. Faulkner right here."

Suddenly George noticed something else and said quickly, "Look over there!" He pointed his flashlight on a shiny object made of steel. The safe in the wall had been crushed, like a soda can. They both went closer. When they examined it more carefully, they noticed something strange. The door of the safe had been completely crushed, like the rest of its steel body; but the wall had not been damaged at all. There was not even one small crack on the wall around the safe.

"How is this possible?" Elena remarked. "There's no explosive or instrument that could have crushed the entire safe this way without damaging the wall."

"Maybe this is the work of the same person who murdered Mr. Faulkner," George responded.

Elena agreed: "It's quite possible."

Then holding the magnifying glass in one hand and the flashlight in the other, she tried to examine the safe more carefully. The flashlight was enough to reveal the strange black symbol at the bottom of the safe, and she did not need to use the magnifying glass. Showing the symbol to George, Elena said, "Doesn't this symbol remind you of something?"

George looked at it and said, "No; it doesn't look at all familiar."

Elena picked up a ballpoint pen and a piece of paper from Mr. Faulkner's desk and told George: "Can you point the flashlight at the bottom of the safe?" She then began to draw the shape of the symbol on the blank sheet of paper. Next, she put the paper in her backpack, picked up the magnifying glass and her flashlight, and looking around at the floor, said: "George, can you carefully search the shelves on the wall and the desk drawers?"

"Alright, certainly," said George. But before he went to check the drawers of Mr. Faulkner's desk, the flashlight in his hand accidentally lit up the top of the desk, and the calendar on the desk caught his eye. Beneath the page on the calendar that showed yesterday's date, something was written that was shining. Out of curiosity, George turned the page of the calendar. He could now see an address that had been written with a yellow fluorescent marker. Below the address was the name of a woman, "Mrs. Smith"; but this name was written with a red magic marker and in a different handwriting. George tore off that page of the calendar and placed it in his pocket. For now, he did not want to bother Elena, who was inspecting the floor of the room. He then went to the drawers of the desk and searched them. Pieces of paper, articles, a few pens, and the many other things in the drawers did not provide George with any clue. Time passed, and then he found a small piece of blue cardboard that seemed familiar to him. He pulled it out from among the papers in the drawer. Even though part of it had been ripped off, George completely recognized this piece of cardboard, which was in fact a piece of the cruise ship ticket, on which the name of the ship and departure time could be seen.

In a subdued voice, George said, "Elena, look at what I found!"

Examining a large brown feather she had picked up off the ground, Elena said, "What? Did you find something?"

George went closer to Elena and, showing her the torn ticket, he stated: "Now I'm certain that there is a link between the murder of Mr. Faulkner and the things that he knew about me."

"But we still don't know what information he had about you," Elena replied.

"We'll soon find out." George said. "Well, what did you find?"

Elena held out the brown feather and responded: "Just this! Of course, it's large enough that I didn't need to use the magnifying glass to find it."

George inspected the feather. "It doesn't seem to be anything important. Mr. Faulkner must have had a bird in his house."

Elena put the feather in a plastic bag and, with the gesture and tone of a professional detective, said: "Things that seem unimportant might be important clues."

Suddenly, flashing red and blue lights shone into the building and began to dance on the wall of the room through the window on the south side. They heard a car brake.

"What is a police car doing here?" Elena wondered. "Maybe one of the neighbors saw the light of our flashlights and reported it to the police."

The word "police" for George reminded him of the word that was on the bulletproof vest of the SWAT team and revived that bitter memory in him. Seriously panicked, he exclaimed: "Maybe it's the police SWAT team; I mean the same person or persons who want to kill me!"

"We parked the car on the north side of the building," Elena said, "so we still have enough time. Hurry up; we have to leave this place as quickly as possible!"

George quickly tossed the backpack on his shoulder, and they both left the room running.

They went through the dark hall and, passing under the yellow ribbons, they promptly got into the car. But as soon as Elena turned the car key and the roaring of the engine was heard, the image of the police car entering the main street from the alley in the back appeared in the side mirror on Elena's side. "Now I'll show them what driving really means!" Elena declared. "George, buckle your seat belt and sit tight! I'm going to show them a real Formula 1 race!"

Elena put on the emergency brake to prevent the car from going forward and floored the gas pedal with her foot. Thick smoke rose from the car tires. Now the orange sports car was like a wild bull, sending dust and debris into the air as it pounded its hooves and prepared itself to attack. When the police car came within five or six meters of them, Elena released the emergency brake, and the car took off like a missile. A few minutes passed, and driving at tremendous speed, Elena glanced in the rearview mirror; but there was no sign of the police car. She looked at George sitting next to her and uttered, "Strange! Why didn't they chase us?"

After a pause, George shrugged his shoulders, opened his eyes wide, and said, "I really don't know!"

"What a pity!" Elena said playfully. "You missed seeing a real car chase. Of course, it was already obvious that I would win!" She then winked at George with her right eye.

But, in fact, why had the police car not followed them? This was the question for which they still had no answer. They went back along the same route through the woods that was full of twists and turns. The moonlight continued to shine, creating a mysterious atmosphere. About an hour later, the sound of the iron door was heard lifting, and the orange car became quiet inside the garage.

They had both become very tired and hungry. For this reason, as George leaned back on one of the leather sofas with his arms and legs dangling down, Elena left the kitchen for the great room with a small tray of food, just two sandwiches and two beverages in glasses. She first put the tray on the table around which the furniture was arranged, and then went to sit on the brown leather sofa next to George.

"Thank you very much!" he said.

Elena smiled and replied: "After an adventure and visiting a ghost house, it's time to recharge our batteries." She then reached for the sandwiches, picked up a ham sandwich, and took a big bite.

George, who seemed very tired, said: "Damn our luck! If the police car had not come, I'm sure we could have found more evidence."

Elena, still chewing, said: "Don't be so sure! If you want to find any evidence, clue, or address, the best place to search is that person's office. And we searched it sufficiently, didn't we?"

As if having remembered something, George stared at a corner and repeated to himself: "The address…the address…that shining address! I totally forgot it."

"What are you talking about?" Elena queried.

George shifted himself on the leather chair in order to stick his hand more easily into his pants pocket, and then took out the page from the calendar, showed it to Elena, and said: "This is the address that I found on Mr. Faulkner's desk. It might be an important clue."

Elena looked at the address and said: "Mrs. Smith! Very good! We will certainly visit Mrs. Smith at this address and ask her a few questions. You got really exhausted today; you need to get a good night's sleep tonight, because tomorrow we've got a lot to do."

Chapter 24

No matter how she tried to move the control lever of the fighter-bomber, it was of no use. The display screen in front of her made her realize that the missiles were keyed in and locked on the target. No matter how she struggled, it was useless, because her thumb was moving involuntarily toward the red button, as though she had no control. The missiles were fired at the target, and the images of the faces of Afghan women and children flashed through her mind. She shouted several times, "No, no, no…," and then she woke up. It was a horrifying nightmare, one that she had had several times before. This was the reason why she had resigned from the military. She did not want to cause the slaughter of innocent human beings because of her mistakes. A cold sweat covered Elena's face. She had taken part in several operations in Afghanistan a few years earlier, and in an aerial bombing, she had succeeded in killing some of the Taliban jihadists. But in one of the operations, the Taliban's base was located in a residential area; and after the bombing, she realized that many innocent human beings had been killed in the course of this attack. Her conscience was still tormenting her. She got out of bed and drank a glass of water. She wiped the sweat off her face and then started walking toward her office.

It was 3:17 AM and moonlight was shining into George's room. George was spread out on the bed in such a deep sleep that waking him seemed out of the question. After all, he had had a very adventurous day.

Looking at the palace from the courtyard, only one light is on; it is Elena's office. She is working on something with great care and precision, focusing the light of the reading lamp on a card with a white background and blue margins. On the left side of the card is a round seal with thirteen small gold stars arranged at equal distances. Most skillfully, Elena glues a photograph of herself on the right side of the card in the middle of which appears three blue letters: "FBI."

Chapter 25

Sunlight had replaced the moonlight. With his eyes closed, George was tossing to one side and then the other, causing the white sheet, part of which covered George's legs and the other part of which was hanging from the bed, to fall to the floor. At this time, someone was knocking at the door and a voice came from behind the door: "George, are you awake? I'll wait for you downstairs so we can have breakfast together. By the way, don't forget, today we have to visit Mrs. Smith."

Between sleep and wakefulness, struggling to wake up and hardly hearing the vague voice, George said, "OK, I'll be there right away."

Elena did not say anything else, and George could only hear the sound of her footsteps getting farther away from the room. A few minutes later, George was walking down the marble steps, and the sound of his shoes hitting the checkered stones was pounding like a sledgehammer on the head of Peter, who was standing near Elena ready to serve at the dining room table. As George came closer, Peter greeted him coldly: "Hello, sir."

"Hello Elena; hello Peter," George said.

Peter, who could not tolerate any strange man addressing the Mistress by her first name, was trying to conceal his irritation and said: "If that is all, I will take my leave, Madam. Call me if you need anything, Madam." Then, holding up his head to avoid looking at George, he went to the kitchen.

George, who did not understand the reason for Peter's behavior, said: "What's wrong with Peter? Does he have a problem with me?"

"It's Peter, after all," Elena said shrugging her shoulders. "He has his own peculiar ways. By the way, did you sleep well last night?"

"I was so tired that as soon as my head hit the pillow, I was out," George said. Then, looking carefully at what Elena was wearing, he said: "Quite a change today! This is the first time I've seen you wear a proper jacket and pants instead of a two-piece bathing suit. By the way, what happened to your swords?"

Elena responded: "We need to go and see Mrs. Smith today. And now you know the reason why I'm dressed this way."

George smiled and said nothing more. They had breakfast together; and as usual, Elena downed her glass of orange juice in one gulp.

About 9:40, the sound of the engine of the orange sports car was heard once again, and George and Elena began their adventure.

This time, they were traveling in the poor areas of the city, the areas where many are afraid to visit after dark. They still did not know the relationship between Mrs. Smith and Mr. Faulkner; but a visit to Mrs. Smith could provide the answer to this question. As the car continued on its way slowly, they were looking intently out the car windows, checking the houses carefully. Elena looked at the calendar page once again, and then put her foot on the brakes with confidence and said, "At last, we're here!" She then looked at George and said: "Before we get out, I would like to make a request of you. Let me speak first, and you just nod your head in approval of what I say occasionally. Agreed?"

Despite the fact that George did not know what plan Elena had in mind, he said, "OK, agreed." George completely trusted Elena, and this sense of trust came from his heart, the same feeling in his heart that he did not know whether to call love or something else.

They emerged from their expensive automobile, and Elena pressed the button of the doorbell of the house. A few moments later, a middle-aged woman cracked open the old door of the house, on which the paint had faded, with the safety chain preventing it from completely opening. Then she cast a suspicious look at Elena and George through the same crack and asked, "Who are you looking for?"

Elena said, "Mrs. Smith?"

The woman was hesitant for a moment: "Who are you?"

Elena stepped forward, taking out a card from the pocket of her black jacket and said firmly: "FBI. We would like to ask you a few questions about the murder of Mr. Faulkner."

The woman looked at the card and said: "I told the police everything I know yesterday."

"Mrs. Smith, we are working exclusively on this case. So, please cooperate with us."

Seeing how serious Elena was, the woman said, "Please, come in!" Her house was simple but orderly and clean, and she had good taste in her arrangement of the furnishings.

Sitting next to George on the old couch, Elena crossed one leg over the other and began by saying: "Mrs. Smith, how well did you know Mr. Faulkner?"

Mrs. Smith, who was sitting across from them, said: "Well, in these ten years that I worked in Mr. Faulkner's house, I got to know him relatively well; and of course, I must say that I know who killed him. I suppose you would like to know too, right?" Elena and George were shocked when they heard this. Mrs. Smith continued: "Mr. Faulkner was murdered by the same peculiar old man who came to his home, keeping an appointment that he had with Mr. Faulkner at 8:00 PM.

They talked together for a while in his office. I'm not certain exactly what they were talking about, but about a half hour later, when I was setting the table, the peculiar old man left the house quickly, but there was no sign of Mr. Faulkner. When I went to the office, I found Mr. Faulkner's body on the floor with a knife pierced deep into his heart. It was really a horrible sight." Then tears began to flow down Mrs. Smith's face. George got up and offered a handkerchief to Mrs. Smith to wipe the tears.

"Had you seen that old man before that night?" Elena asked.

Wiping her tears, Mrs. Smith said in a trembling voice, "No, never."

"Then why do you say that the old man was peculiar?"

"His very long white beard," Mrs. Smith replied, "the black cloak he was wearing, the cone-shaped hat that looked like a trumpet on his head, and the large eagle with brown wings and a white head that was sitting on the old man's shoulder were all peculiar to me."

"During the time that the old man and Mr. Faulkner were in the office, did you hear any loud noise, such as an explosion?" Elena inquired.

"No, I did not."

"When you entered the office, was the door to the safe open?"

"Even though I was quite shocked at seeing the body," Mrs. Smith replied, "I noticed the crushed door of the safe."

"Then, the door of the safe was open?"

"Yes, it was wide open," Mrs. Smith answered.

"What did Mr. Faulkner keep in his safe?"

"Well, he kept his most valuable possessions there."

"Could you explain a little more explicitly?"

Mrs. Smith said: "As you know, after the death of Albert Einstein, Thomas Stoltz Harvey, a physician at Princeton Hospital, sectioned Albert Einstein's brain into hundreds of slivers and mounted them on microscope slides. Well, after many years, Mr. Faulkner was able to acquire one of these valuable slides to carry out a series of studies. In fact, the slide that he had was a unique one, and he kept it in the safe, that same safe that is now crushed."

"Just one more question," Elena added. She then took out the piece of paper on which she had drawn the strange symbol from the pocket of the jacket, and holding it before Mrs. Smith, asked: "Do you recognize this symbol?"

Mrs. Smith squinted to see better and, carefully looking at the symbol, said after few moments: "No, I do not recognize this symbol. This is the first time I have seen it."

"Thank you very much for cooperating with us." Elena said. "I have no further questions."

But before Elena could stand up, George interrupted. "I still have a few more questions. Was Mr. Faulkner supposed to go on a trip? For instance, on a vacation?"

Mrs. Smith said: "No, he was not supposed to go on a trip. Whenever he wanted to travel, he would let me know at least one week in advance."

"We found your address on Mr. Faulkner's desk calendar," George said. "If you have been working for him for ten years, why did he need to write your address on his calendar?"

Mrs. Smith answered: "He had not written my address. I wrote my address on the calendar. In fact, I moved to this place about five days ago, and Mr. Faulkner asked me to write my new address for him. That's all."

"How did you know what Mr. Faulkner kept in his safe?"

"Mr. Faulkner neither had a wife nor any children." Mrs. Smith responded. "What's more, he completely trusted me. That is why he sometimes had a heart-to-heart talk with me, and would even tell me his secrets. Of course, since I am a person who keeps secrets well, if it weren't because of the investigation about Mr. Faulkner's murder, I would never have told you these things, sir."

Obviously, Mrs. Smith was offended by what George had said; but in any case, George asked his last question: "Do you know another secret regarding Mr. Faulkner that you have not told us?"

"No, sir," Mrs. Smith replied coldly. "I've told you everything I know."

George took a deep breath and said: "Well, thank you very much for cooperating with us." Then he and Elena stood up and left through the same door they had come in a few minutes earlier. They had not gotten into the car yet when George asked: "Wait a minute! Are you also an FBI agent?"

"George, that card was a fake," Elena said.

"What if she had figured it out?"

"You didn't figure out that it was a fake. Besides, I'm good at what I do."

George, who felt that arguing with Elena was useless, preferred just to get into the car. Once again, the roaring of the engine was heard and they headed towards home. As she was shifting gears, Elena asked, "Do you think she was lying?"

"No," George responded. "In fact, in my opinion, everything she said was the truth. You could tell from her eyes."

Elena said: "I also think she was being honest in her answers to the questions. But, who is that peculiar old man whose footprints show up in everything that happens? How could he have traveled so quickly to have been present at all the events in the course of one night?"

"I have no clue. Maybe he flew like a missile and…"

Before George could finish his sentence, Elena suddenly hit the brakes so hard that if George had not buckled his seat belt, he would have been thrown through the windshield. The ear-piercing sound of the breaks resonated in the air.

"What are you doing?" George asked.

They heard the continuous sound of the horns of the cars behind them, as he drivers were shaking their fists in protest; but ignoring all this and before saying anything, Elena turned the steering wheel, put her foot on the gas pedal, and turning the car around, said, "Why didn't I think of it sooner?" Thick smoke rose in the air behind the car tires, and now the car was moving in the opposite direction on the street.

"Could you possibly tell me what's going on?" George questioned.

Preparing herself to pass the car in front of her, Elena said, "Do you remember the newspaper on the ship?"

George looked at her in surprise and asked, "What do you mean?"

Elena answered: "Some people have claimed that on the night that all these events occurred, they saw a flying creature in the sky, a flying creature that was carrying a very large object on its back."

"Wait a minute!" George said. "Do you mean that the old man was using that flying creature?"

"Yes, this is exactly what I mean."

"Now where are you going in such a hurry?"

"There is a military base nearby," Elena said. "They might be able to reveal to us the nature of this flying creature and its source and destination, given what they have recorded on their radar."

Chapter 26

Standing in such a way as to avoid his shiny shoes being stained by blood, he was looking at the body of a man of about sixty-five years of age. He put his hand in his jacket pocket; he really wanted to smoke a cigar. Then he immediately remembered the promise he had made to himself. After the bitter incident that had happened many years ago, he had made a pledge to himself never to smoke on duty, especially at a murder scene. So, he instantaneously pulled back his hand and resisted the temptation to smoke. He paused, thinking for a little while; and when he turned his head, he noticed the safe that was built into the wall. He had not taken more than a few steps when the reflection of a yellow light made him stop. He went to the desk. He turned the page of the calendar. An address was written with yellow fluorescent marker, but it was unclear whose address it was. No name had been written on that page. He memorized the address. He had never been one to take notes. Then he went to the crushed safe in the opposite wall. A strange symbol in black was evident at the bottom of the safe. He looked at it with curiosity and then said in a loud voice, "Officer Williams!"

Immediately, a young man appeared behind him: "Yes, sir!"

"Take a picture of this **symbol** right away and send it to the decoding team!" the detective said.

Chapter 27

The orange car left behind several other cars as well, and gradually a concrete wall that stretched for hundreds of meters appeared to their right. The coiled barbed wire at the top of the concrete wall indicated that this was a security zone. The sports car took a side road that led to the military air base and stopped in front of the inspection station. Elena took out another card from her pocket and showed it to a corpulent man in military uniform. The man looked at the card, then at Elena's face, and then nodding in approval he said loudly, "You may pass." The barrier gate arm about a meter from the ground began to rise on its base, and the way was opened to them. The car advanced on an asphalt road until they arrived at a massive, tall concrete building some twelve or thirteen stories high. On the top of the building, a gigantic radar antenna was rotating. A little further on, very large satellite dishes mounted on huge high metal bases pointed toward the sky, and large metal warehouses that undoubtedly were used to store military airplanes came into view.

They climbed the stairs. Once again, Elena showed her card, to the two armed guards standing in front of the entrance to the building, and they finally passed into the concrete building. She pressed a button on the wall next to a shiny metal door. The elevator door opened, and then she pressed another button, number 10. The elevator door closed slowly, and it began to ascend speedily. It took no more than thirty seconds before they heard a short beep and the door opened to a long hallway. Numerous rooms lined both sides of the hallway.

Elena raised her left eyebrow and said to herself: "If I'm not mistaken, it was room number 7." Then they began to walk under the lights that lit the hallway, as their shadows became shorter, then longer. As they were advancing along the hallway, they also looked at the numbers of the rooms: 2, 1, 3…7. Elena knocked on the door and then turned the metal handle. When the door to the room opened, the two men who were sitting at the computer systems turned their eyes from the black display screen on which a green line was moving in circles toward the door. One of them, who had brown hair and thick glasses, stood up, and with a smile on his face as if going to greet his old friend, walked toward George and Elena. Elena ran to him and said, "Arthur!" They embraced for a few moments. "I cannot tell you how happy I am to see you," Elena said.

"I'm happy to see you, too!" Arthur replied. "I haven't heard from you for a long time. By the way, who is this handsome guy with you?"

Elena said, "Oh, I forgot to introduce you two." Then pointing to George, she said, "My friend, George," and then pointing to Arthur, she said: "Arthur is my old friend and colleague. I've learned a great deal from him." After George and Arthur warmly shook hands and exchanged smiles as a sign of respect, Elena continued: "Arthur, I'd like you to do something for me."

"What can I do for you?" Arthur asked.

"I would like to know whether or not you picked up anything strange two nights ago, between 8:00 and 9:00, or around that time. Or did anything strange happen in the sky around here?"

Arthur paused for a moment. "Of course, what I'm going to tell you must stay strictly between us," he said. "To tell you the truth, two nights ago, we identified a suspicious flying object on our radar, flying at approximately a 70-degree angle from the surface of the ground. We even dispatched two fighter-bombers for further investigation; but the pilots did not find anything, as though that object had become invisible. Some minutes later, the image of the object even disappeared from our radar screens. We were quite confused ourselves; and for this reason, we sent the coordinates of the movement and the recorded specifications of that flying object to the Space Studies Institute. They took numerous pictures of the route of the object in the sky for us. Several photographs were taken by the space telescopes; but unfortunately, we have not reached a conclusion yet, and the nature of that flying object is in a cloud of ambiguity. By the way, how did you find out about this, since due to security issues, this news has not been leaked yet?"

"It's a long story," Elena said. "I'll tell you all about it later. I would only like to ask you to e-mail me the photographs sent to you by the Space Studies Institute. I might be able to help you solve this puzzle."

"No problem," Arthur replied. "Just give me your e-mail address; I'll send them all to you."

"Do you have a pen and a piece of paper?"

"I'll get them right away."

Chapter 28

After thanking Arthur and bidding him farewell, Elena and George once again got into their iron horse, and the roaring of the car engine was heard. Their adventure today appeared to be completed; however, new incidents were yet awaiting them.

When they arrived home, as they were climbing the stairs from the garage, Peter came to greet them: "Madam, you have a guest. Mr. Hopkins has come to see you. He does not appear to be well, and even though I told him that the Mistress is not here, he preferred to wait until you came back, Madam. I think he has some very important business with you. I took him to the great room; but since his arrival, he has not even sat down for a moment and has been constantly pacing back and forth in the hall, Madam." Perhaps what caused Peter to talk so much was that Mr. Hopkins was not feeling well.

"Thank you very much, Peter," Elena responded.

Peter took a short bow and left.

Walking toward the hall, Elena told George: "It's Thomas Hopkins. He's Mrs. Hopkins' only son. You remember Mrs. Hopkins, the history professor?"

"Yes, I remember. But what is her son doing here?"

"We'll soon find out."

The shadow of Mr. Hopkins was moving back and forth on the wall of the great room like a clock pendulum. He was quite restless. Obviously, something had caused him to be distraught. But what?

Several meters away from Mr. Hopkins, Elena said: "Hello, Thomas! I'm so happy to see you."

Upon hearing Elena's voice, Mr. Hopkins stopped in his tracks, looked at George and Elena, and with his face showing a mixture of sadness, anger, frustration, and confusion, he said hurriedly: "Hello Elena. Your number was the last number that my mother called. I would like to know what she told you." The way he spoke more resembled that of an interrogator than a guest. Better stated, he was talking like a criminal investigator.

Surprised by Thomas' restlessness and discomfort, Elena's face changed. "Has something happened?" she said.

This question was like cold water poured over Thomas, as if his soul were frozen for a moment. No longer able to stand on his legs, he collapsed on one of the leather sofas, and while trying to control his feelings and prevent his tears, he took several deep breaths and pressed his lips together. He sighed. He was silent for a moment; and then he explained the dreadful incident that was tormenting him:

"Yesterday afternoon when I returned home, I faced a horrifying scene. I found the bodies of my father and mother on the ground, with a sword pierced into the heart of each. Last night, I spent a very bad night in a hotel. I was so upset that I couldn't sleep all night. But today, something crossed my mind, and I went back home and checked the numbers recorded on the telephone and realized that here was the number to which my mother had made her last call. Elena, you are the only one who can help me." Then a teardrop began to roll down his face.

The shock evident on her face, Elena said, "Oh, my God! I can't believe it!"

"Elena, what did my mother say in her last telephone call to you?" Thomas asked. "This is very important to me." Thomas' sad eyes showed some sort of insistence on finding the truth.

With a lump in her throat, Elena said: "When your mother called me, I was not at home, so, she left me a message. We can go upstairs and listen to the telephone message."

"No, I'm not ready for it now," Thomas said, distraught. "Hearing my mother's voice when she is no longer alive would really drive me crazy. Just tell me what her message was about."

"She said that she had made a new discovery in connection with Nostradamus and…"

Elena had not finished speaking when Thomas interrupted her: "No, that's not what I mean. I only want to know if my mother said anything about The Organization. Of course, a long time has passed since that story, but it's possible that that damned Organization ordered the murder of my parents."

Elena was trying hard not to cry; but eventually tears began to well up in her eyes. She remembered the time when she had lost her mother. She did not want to cry as she had then; she knew that crying was of no use. Hence, she was trying to hold back the tears that had welled up in her eyes by thinking about something else. Yes, she was thinking about revenge. So, using all her strength to overcome her emotions, she said: "Which organization are you talking about? What are you saying?"

Before Thomas could answer, George tried to calm the situation a little. Handing each of them a tissue to wipe their tears, he asked them to set aside the questions and answers, even if for only a few seconds. On George's request, the servant brought two glasses of cold water. Thomas took a sip, leaned his neck back on the cushion of the leather sofa, and for some moments, he thought about the past and reminisced. He sighed once again, and this time he began to speak more calmly, answering the question that Elena had asked a few moments earlier:

"Well, obviously, my mother had not mentioned anything about this to you. This issue goes back to twenty-seven years ago, when I was only five years old. As you know, my father was a genetic scientist. He helped a research organization with animal cloning. Eventually, a number of the members of The Organization decided to use this capability for human cloning as well. Before long, this idea was strongly opposed by a group of politicians, religious leaders, and, in particular, the Pope, and even other well-known figures. None of the organizations that were working on cloning had legal permission to do human cloning. But twenty-seven years ago, a strange incident occurred. One night, my father woke up terrified. He had dreamt that a young man with white feathered wings growing from his two shoulders came down to earth from the sky. The young man was wearing a very long, white, spotless gown and was very handsome. He introduced himself to my father in these words: 'I am the Lord's Special Angel, and I have a command for you from my Creator.' He then showed some small glass bottles to my father and continued: 'You must clone a human using that which is inside these bottles to create a human that is different from all other human beings, a warrior who will fight only for God. A great war will occur in a remote location. That which I have said to you is the Lord's command.' He then opened his white wings and flew into the sky. The next morning, when my father went to The Organization, he saw those exact small bottles on his desk. He had become convinced that this was a Divine mission that had to be carried out. From then on, he secretly worked on this project until he finally succeeded in cloning a human. My father brought home the cloned infant; but two weeks later, on a cold moonlit night, another strange thing happened. My mother had gone to the kitchen to prepare a baby bottle of milk for the infant. When she went back to the room, despite the fact that she had not turned on the light, in the moonlight, she could see an old man with a long white beard, in a black cloak and tall cone-shaped hat, standing in the middle of the room with the infant in his arms. Horrified, my mother screamed loudly, and the old man, still holding the infant, broke the window, jumped out, and disappeared in a matter of minutes. If anyone had known that my father had created a human clone, the entire Organization would have been in trouble, and several million dollars in funding for The Organization would have been cut off forever. Of course, sometime later, The Organization secretly proposed that my father work on a project for the military; but he did not agree to it, and he resigned three months later and left The Organization. I never learned what the proposed military project was, but I have a feeling that the members of The Organization killed my parents and..."

As Thomas was speaking, George placed his fingers on his temples for a few moments; but he tried to make certain that the others did not notice his headache. Parts of what Thomas had said had once again made those vague images return, bringing on another severe headache for George for a few moments.

Thomas was still talking when suddenly his cell phone rang. He excused himself for a few moments; and when his telephone call ended, his face changed. "They called from the Police Department and asked me to go there," he said. "Apparently, they have found new information." He then got up.

"Let me know if you find out anything!" Elena said.

"Certainly," was Thomas' reply. Then he hugged Elena, shook hands with George, and left for the Police Department.

Chapter 29

Stepping out of the black car with his right foot first, he slammed the car door shut, and crushed his cigar, half-smoked, under his shiny shoes. Sticking his chest out, he walked toward the crowd. The young man who was following him walked past him quickly to the crowd and, pushing the people aside, said, "Clear the way; let Detective Anderson in!"

With his stealthy, sharp eyes, the detective looked at the young man and said: "Officer Williams! While I take a look inside the building, check out the outside around the house; see if you find anything suspicious."

Williams said, "Yes, sir!" He held the yellow plastic ribbon up, and they quickly passed under it. They inspected everything carefully, from the protruded carvings on the wooden door of the house to the hallway light. A round wooden table was in the center of the room, on which a striking blue vase filled with a bouquet of dried red carnations could be seen. Four brown wooden chairs were on the four sides of the table. An old French chandelier provided light for the large room, and a few small rugs were scattered across the floor of the room in no particular order. Paintings of ancient Egypt, much like the drawings found on the walls inside the Egyptian pyramids, were hanging on the wall. A number of historians believe that Nostradamus acquired his power of prophecy at the pyramids of

Egypt; but whether or not these drawings had any connection with this issue, that was a question that could only be answered by Mrs. Hopkins.

The policeman who was standing at attention inside the great room directed the detective to the room in question. When he entered the room, he saw the bodies of a middle-aged couple with two swords pierced deeply into their hearts. The detective looked at a man in a white gown who was examining the corpses and asked, "What is the time of death?"

The medical examiner stared at him from over the rim of his glasses and, exhaling, said: "Twelve to fourteen hours have elapsed since they died." Then standing up, he began to remove his gloves and continued: "If you want a more precise time, you'll have to wait until tomorrow morning. Of course, I will begin the autopsy tonight. By the way, the fingerprinting team took fingerprints from the knife with which Professor Faulkner was killed. I saw the results just a couple of hours ago. Only the fingerprints of Professor Faulkner could be found on the handle of the knife."

Calmly and unemotionally, the detective said, "Thanks, Doc." He thought for a moment and then mumbled to himself, "No way they committed suicide." He then turned his head to a policeman in the great room and said, "What information do you have so far?"

The young man said: "The bodies are those of Mr. and Mrs. Hopkins." Then pointing to a red suitcase placed next to the wall, holding an airline ticket in his hand, he walked slowly forward and continued: "As we have figured out, Mrs. Hopkins was supposed to fly to France, to Paris, today. We found this ticket in her suitcase." He then handed the ticket to the detective.

The detective looked at the ticket, raised his eyebrows, and said: "We have to find out why she was going to France."

Concentrating, the detective closed his eyes for a few minutes. He finally opened his eyes and carefully looked around at everything, including the history books and the antique objects that filled the shelves, as well as the paintings on the walls. The thing that was most intriguing to him as a detective was the poster on the wall, the same poster that showed the scene of the collision of an airplane with a tall tower. This poster seemed out of sync with the other things in the room, and this seemed odd to him. He looked at the poster for a few moments, and then he turned his head. The waving curtain that was halfway drawn in front of the window caught his attention. Forcefully, he drew the curtain aside. Outside the window on the ground, red carnations were slowly swaying in the mild breeze. He stared from behind the windowpane at the other side of the street. Squinting a little, he said to himself, "Number 54."

He then set off immediately. He left the house and found Officer Williams searching the shrubbery around the house. The detective asked, "Did you find anything?"

"No, sir!" Williams responded.

The detective said, "Come with me!" Some seconds later, the images of the two were reflected on the brass number 54 on the outside wall of the house. Officer Williams rang the bell, and a man of about 40 years of age opened the door. The detective took out a card from his pocket and said: "I'm Detective Anderson from the Criminal Division. I would like to ask you a few questions about the murder of Mr. and Mrs. Hopkins."

The man dropped his head and said in a sad tone: "It was really a horrible incident. Yes, of course."

The detective explained: "Given the position of your house, you have a better view of Mr. and Mrs. Hopkins' house than any of the other neighbors. Did you notice anything out of the ordinary today? Did you see a person or persons enter their house?"

The man thought for a moment and then said: "No, I didn't see anything suspicious. When I was leaving my house to go to work this morning, I saw Mr. Hopkins, who was picking a bouquet of flowers from in front of the window of his house. I greeted him and said good morning, and he was very congenial and said good morning to me. Everything seemed completely normal."

"May I talk to the other people in the house?" the detective asked. "They might have seen something."

"But I live here alone."

"Did Mr. or Mrs. Hopkins have any enemies?"

"Not as far as I know," the man responded. "They were nice people who didn't bother anyone."

"Do you know why Mrs. Hopkins wanted to take a trip to Paris today?"

The man said, "I have no idea."

"Thank you very much." Detective Anderson said. "I have no more questions for now." On his way back, Detective Anderson stopped for a moment, and gazing at the carnations, he said, "That's very odd!"

Williams asked, "What is odd, sir?"

Detective Anderson said: "How is it possible for flowers that were picked recently to dry within about fourteen hours? The carnations on the table in the middle of the great room were completely dry. That is really strange!"

Chapter 30

One day had passed, and still there was no news of Thomas. Elena was restless, and now that Thomas had left and was no longer pacing back and forth in the hall, Elena was doing it instead. She suddenly stopped, and in a tone that was both upset and angry, she said: "This damned puzzle has to be solved. I have to find out how these incidents are related. I will catch this murderer!" Then, she said nothing more and resolutely set off for the stairs.

George asked, "Where are you going?"

Continuing on her way, Elena said: "I need to listen to Mrs. Hopkins' telephone message one more time. I might find some clues."

George also stood up and following Elena said: "Perhaps we should both listen to that message together once again." The sound of their climbing the stairs resonated in the hall.

Resting her chin on her elbow, in a posture appearing very much like a criminal detective inspecting a crime scene, Elena was staring at the telephone. The extended beep was heard from the telephone at the end of the telephone message. Elena looked at George and asked, "Did you figure out anything?"

George, who was standing with his arms folded on his chest in the middle of the room, sighed and said:

"This is the fifth time we've listened to this message. If there was any clue in connection with the murder of Mr. and Mrs. Hopkins, we should have figured it out by now, don't you think?"

Elena, who was sitting on top of her desk, jumped down and, pacing around the room, was trying to put all her information together. She said: "Let's go back over all the events from the beginning together! Mr. and Mrs. Hopkins and Mr. Faulkner were all three murdered in the same way; and Mrs. Smith says that the same old man in black murdered Mr. Faulkner. If we assume that all three were murdered by the same person, then the murderer of Mr. and Mrs. Hopkins also has to be that same old man dressed in black."

"But one thing is not right here," George said. "Mr. Faulkner knew about me, and we were supposed to meet on that cruise ship. So, if after the murder of Mr. Faulkner their intention was to kill me, that morning, instead of the police SWAT team, that strange old man should have entered my house to kill me."

"By the way, do you remember the address of that house?" Elena asked. "We might be able to find new clues."

"At that moment, the only thing that I thought about was how to stay alive," George responded. "I don't even quite remember how I escaped, let alone the address of that place."

"Then we must solve the puzzle with the information that we have available to us," Elena posited.

George said, "Maybe Thomas was right."

"What do you mean?"

George, who was trying to be more methodical in his reasoning, said: "Both Mr. Faulkner and Mr. Hopkins worked in genetics. Maybe they were working on a secret project; or maybe in fact they wanted to prevent a secret project from being carried out and were going to disclose some information and that's why they were murdered by The Organization."

Opening the window, Elena said: "However, in my opinion, this theory cannot be correct. If a modern, advanced organization with hundreds of millions of dollars in funding decided to murder two well-known genetic scientists, it would do it quietly, for instance, in a fake automobile accident, using toxins, or in the most extreme case, it would hire a professional hit man to finish the job with one bullet, and not hire a swordsman."

"I guess you're right," George admitted. They both sank into thought for a few minutes, until George broke the silence, and this time, he raised a different question: "Maybe Mr. Faulkner did not know me at all. Mrs. Smith, who worked there for ten years, when she was face to face with me, treated me like a stranger.

This means that in the course of these ten years, I had not gone to Mr. Faulkner's house even once. And if I was not that close to Mr. Faulkner, to have at least visited his home a few times, then why should he risk his life for me and make an appointment with me? Of course, perhaps Mr. Faulkner and I were not supposed to meet on the ship. Mrs. Smith said that Mr. Faulkner was not supposed to go on a trip. Or, perhaps he intended to do something like we did after getting on the ship, and he returned home in his private helicopter, which of course, seems unlikely. I don't think that Mr. Faulkner had a private helicopter."

Gesturing in protest, Elena slowly shook her head to one side and then the other, with her eyes wide open, and in response to each statement she said "perhaps," "but," or "if"! Then with her hands on the window frame facing the courtyard, she took a deep breath of fresh air to calm down. George continued to stand in the middle of the room without saying a word. Elena turned her head, looked at George, and said: "I apologize! But, George, these conjectures don't solve any problem. Didn't you find the cruise ship ticket in Mr. Faulkner's desk drawer? Didn't you say that on finding the ticket you are now certain? Look, George, this puzzle might be much more complicated than we even think! We do not have all the information we need to solve this puzzle. And that is why the more we think, the more we find contradictions, and the more confused we become. But we can solve this puzzle through another method, or I should say, instead of solving the puzzle ourselves, we can make use of someone else to solve the puzzle, the person at whom all the paths end and who can provide us with sufficient information."

"I don't know what you mean!" said George.

Elena explained: "When you want to solve a puzzle, you have to look at it from a distance; and you don't need to know all the details from the beginning. If you look at all the incidents that have occurred in the past few days from a distance, what do you see? Mrs. Hopkins was murdered after she found out a big secret in connection with Nostradamus. We also know that the skull of Nostradamus was stolen; and the skulls of Merce Cunningham, Michelangelo, Blackbeard, Beethoven, and Shakespeare were also stolen on that same night. And who is the person the eyewitnesses saw around those graves before the skulls were stolen? Who kidnapped the cloned infant from the home of Mr. and Mrs. Hopkins? Who was the person who killed Mr. Faulkner? The footprints of that old man in black are evident in all these incidents. We might not know all the details, but what we do know is that all these incidents lead to him. So, we have to concentrate on only one thing. We have to find that old man dressed in black."

Elena's argument had completely convinced George. Nevertheless, he raised another question: "But where are we supposed to look for this old man?"

Elena suddenly got up and went to her laptop, which was on the other side of the desk, and said: "Good thing you asked that! I had totally forgotten about Arthur. He must have sent the photographs to me by now. For now, our only hope for finding the old man is these photographs."

About an hour had passed since Elena had turned on her laptop screen, and the two were still looking at the screen most intently. Finally, George stretched his neck, and trying to prevent himself from yawning said: "They all look alike. I don't see any clues or signs in these thirteen photographs. I think that..." Suddenly, George became silent without finishing what he was saying.

"What happened?" Elena asked. "You were saying..."

George brought his head closer to Elena and said quietly, "Look at the edge of the window!" The thing that had surprised George was an eagle with a white head and brown wings that was carefully scrutinizing the inside of their room with its sharp eyes, holding tightly to the window frame with its strong claws.

Elena stood up slowly and moved toward the eagle. When she had reached close enough, slowly she pulled away from it the old pieces of rolled up paper that the eagle was holding in its yellow beak. She was now holding two pieces of old paper in her hands; but the papers were of different types. The eagle, which had successfully completed its mission, turned away from them, opened its large wings and flew off; and after a few moments, it was a dot in the sky. As Elena was unrolling the old pieces of paper, slowly and with great curiosity, George came to her side. But George was unable to read the writing on the first piece of paper, because the writing was a mixture of Greek, Italian, and Latin.

The smell of old paper had filled the room; and as Elena was amazingly translating the sentences in her mind, like an archaeologist, she whispered: "Century VII, Quatrain 43: The night will come, the night when an army of prophets clad in white, like chess figures, confronts an army of wizards clad in black, and the battle will begin for which they have been waiting for thousands of years; yet, a greater battle is underway." At the end of this quatrain, a strange black symbol could be seen that looked almost exactly like the symbol at the bottom of Mr. Faulkner's safe. After Elena finished reading the quatrain, she pondered for moment.

Looking at her, George asked, "What language are these writings in?"

Elena, who was staring at the piece of paper and seemed to be remembering something, said, "Nostradamus."

Surprised, George said, "Nostradamus! What do you mean?"

Suddenly, as if having discovered something, Elena shouted with excitement: "Nostradamus! Oh, my God! These are the missing prophecies of Nostradamus!"

"How can you be so sure?" George asked.

Her eyes still sparkling with joy and her voice shaking with excitement, Elena said: "I have seen his handwriting before. A few months ago, Mrs. Hopkins showed me some writing that was written by Nostradamus personally." Then, without giving George the chance to ask anything else, she eagerly began reading the remaining prophecies: "44: The final battle will occur in front of the gate of the gods, fiery anchors shall twirl in the sky to destroy its columns, a harsh battle shall begin in the sea and sky, the great tower shall be set in flight in the sky. 45: Sea fairies shall sing, swamp fairies shall dance, the forces of white and black shall be combined, angels of death shall be hindered from advancement. 46: The old man in black shall drag the bones from under the earth, he will disappear among the stars, he will enter the dark hole, the same place where the greatest battle of the entire universe shall begin."

The 46th quatrain completely transfixed Elena and George. These quatrains held two very important clues. First, at the end of each quatrain, the same strange symbol was engraved that they had seen in the house of Mr. Faulkner; and second, quatrain 46 described precisely the incident that had occurred two nights earlier. Elena, who had become very enthusiastic, checked the next piece of paper to read the rest of the quatrains; but the second piece of paper had no similarity at all to the first. But that which was the source of their astonishment was not the material of the papers. Rather, the difference was in something else. The difference was in the words that could be seen on the second piece of paper, words that even George could read:

"Would you like to read quatrain 47, and the rest of the quatrains as well? Then, you must look for me, because I am the only person who has the missing quatrains. However, I do not think that you have enough time, because you are weak creatures and your planet will soon be destroyed. Hence, rather than looking for me, you should prepare yourselves for death."

No more than a few seconds had passed after reading the sentences when Elena was so angry that she bit her lower lip, and wadding up the piece of paper in her fist, in a voice that shook with anger, she said: "I will catch this damned old man, wherever he is." She then threw the crushed piece of paper into the trashcan that was in the corner of the room and said: "We don't have much time. We have to find that old man before another incident happens." George continued to stand in silence, looking at Elena. Trying to get hold of herself and concentrate, Elena sank into thought, and in a pose like a detective, she said: "A dark hole among the stars! Does this mean that the old man in black has entered the dark hole among the stars? What does he mean? In fact, exactly where is that dark hole?" After Elena and George thought for a few seconds, something sparked in Elena's mind and she said, "It has to be a black hole in space."

"What the heck is a black hole in space?" George asked.

Elena went to the bookshelf, struggled to pull out a thick book from among the other books, which caused the other books to be disturbed and the rest of the books to collapse like dominoes, leaning toward the left side of the shelf. Elena shrugged her shoulders and raised her eyebrows saying, "Hmmm! I'll arrange them later." Then holding the book and turning the pages, she walked to George. On the back cover of the book was a picture of the sky full of stars, in which all the most brilliant stars that were more visible had been connected together with dotted lines, in such a way that they resembled the image of a bear. She turned the pages of the book until she reached page 417. Then, moving her finger in a zigzag fashion on the page, she stopped her finger on the third paragraph of that page. She said:

"Here it is! Spherical black hole! Read this to see what I mean!"

George held the book calmly and read the following sentences carefully:

"Various stars of different masses might form into white dwarfs or neutron stars; but another occurrence is also possible with regard to such dying stars. If the remaining nuclear mass after a new stellar cloud, supernova, or even hyper nova explosion has three times the mass of the sun, in that case, a continuous gravitational collapse will occur, such that the other basic structures of the material also will not be able to withstand it. Such a star implodes to the point that its mass reaches close to zero. In that case, the density of that point in space-time is infinite. Of course, whenever in a region of space-time sufficient material exists and is concentrated suddenly, again, a black hole is formed. Schwarzschild discovered that if the radius of a mass becomes sufficiently small, its surrounding space-time curves tremendously, and we can assume the gravity resulting from it to be very high, even infinite. In this situation, nothing, not even light, is able to escape from it! As you can see, in Schwarzchild's radius, something strange happens. It seems that clocks work in infinity, and a message that is transmitted in a specific moment in time, for example, 't,' does not reach a more distant radius unless time passes infinitely. In fact, signals that are sent in a radius smaller than a

Schwarzschild radius never escape. Hence, a high mass object that is entirely within the Schwarzschild radius does not radiate to the rest of the world and appears invisible. Such objects are black holes. The inside of such an object is as separate from us as though it is in fact another world."

Now George had learned something. At least he learned the theory that another world exists inside a black hole, a completely different world! Such a world could be so different that it would totally reverse Albert Einstein's laws. George closed the book, and as he was placing it on the desk, he said, "Very interesting! A spherical black hole!"

Elena said, "But where is this black hole located?"

George took a deep breath through his mouth, filling his lungs, quickly puffing up his cheeks with the air that he was blowing out through his puckered lips, and in a tone of exhaustion indicating he could not come up with anything else, he said: "We should let our brains rest a bit, don't you think?"

At this time, there was a knock on the door, and then Peter said: "Pardon me, Madam! Two men have come from the Police Department, and they would like to see you."

George looked at Elena with concern. The word "police" still was associated with the laser gun in his mind.

"Alright, Peter," Elena said. "Tell them to wait for few moments, and I will be there."

"Do you think they have come here to kill me?" George wanted to know.

"Maybe it has something to do with the other night," Elena said, "the night that we were coming back from Mr. Faulkner's house."

George asked, "What should we do now?"

Elena picked up a guitar case from the corner of the room, placed her swords in it, and closed the zipper. She hung the strap of the case over her shoulder and then said: "You stay right here! I'll go downstairs to see what's going on."

Involuntarily, he grabbed Elena's hand and said: "I'll come with you; I can't let you go by yourself."

Elena could see something in George's eyes that more than anything else revealed a sense of concern. George's fondness for her was now visible in his eyes. She held George's hand warmly in her own and said: "Don't worry a bit. I promise you that nothing will happen to me. I'll be back soon." She then smiled at George and walked toward the stairs.

Chapter 31

As he was walking in the hallway, Detective Anderson looked at his face and said: "Officer Williams! Your eyes are very puffy. Obviously, you didn't have enough sleep last night."

Officer Williams pulled down the skin below is left eye and said: "Yes, sir. I couldn't sleep last night, because my mother had turned on an Italian-language network that was broadcasting the funeral ceremonies directly from the Vatican, and she was watching it almost all night, until morning."

The detective looked at him surprised and asked, "What funeral ceremonies are you talking about?"

Officer Williams answered: "Two nights ago, a special aid to the Pope, who was at the time working in the archives of the Vatican, died of a heart attack. Last night, an Italian-language network was broadcasting the funeral ceremonies live. You know my mother, she's a staunch Catholic and watches anything related to the Vatican, and she turns the volume up very high."

The detective said: "That is precisely why I keep telling you that you should live on your own. What's really weird is that at the age of 35, you're still living with your mother!"

The images of Detective Anderson and Officer Williams began to form on the shiny metal door of one of the morgues of the Office of the Medical Examiner as they were entering the room. The walls in the room were tiled in small green tiles. Tossing a bloodstained scalpel into a container, Dr. Maurice said with a smile, "Hello, Detective. At last, you came!" Then he got up from his office chair with casters, which was behind the autopsy table.

"Hello, Doc," the detective greeted. "You had left me a message saying that you have something important to tell me. Have you found a new clue?"

The doctor said: "The first bit of news is that the fingerprinting team examined both swords; but they got strange results. I can tell you that the killer of Mr. and Mrs. Hopkins…"

He had not finished talking when Detective Anderson completed Dr. Morris's sentence: "Is not the same as the murderer of Professor Faulkner. In fact, Mr. and Mrs. Hopkins were killed by someone else."

"Yes, you're right." the doctor replied. "This was one bit of news that I wanted to tell you. But how did you figure this out?"

"Well, it was obvious from the very beginning," the detective said. "It's true that the home of Mr. and Mrs. Hopkins resembles a museum, but the swords did not belong there. Given that Professor Faulkner was killed before they were, why did the murderer not take his swords with him to Faulkner's house but, rather, killed Professor Faulkner with the professor's letter opener that was on his desk? I think that Mr. Faulkner's murder was not premeditated, but the murder of Mr. and Mrs. Hopkins was premeditated. And for this reason, the killer did not take the swords with him."

The doctor smiled and said: "Your reasoning is sound. I came to that same conclusion, based on the evidence that I found. But I wanted you to come here so I could tell you about much more important things. I have much more significant news for you. Mr. and Mrs. Hopkins were not killed with swords." He paused for a moment, and then continued: "Could you pick up the magnifying glass on my desk and come with me? I need to show you something."

Officer Williams picked up the magnifying glass and followed him. The doctor pulled the levered handle of one of morgue's cold chambers, opened the door, and pulled out the drawer. He then unzipped the black plastic body bag and said: "I'm sure you recognize this corpse; it is Mr. Hopkins. Detective, could you look at the neck of the corpse through the magnifying glass?"

The detective took the magnifying glass from Officer Williams and examined the neck of the corpse carefully. Two holes a few centimeters apart were evident on the neck. Dr. Maurice said: "Two holes of precisely the same size are also on Mrs. Hopkins' neck. In fact, some of the bones of the necks of Mr. and Mrs.

Hopkins are broken, and their spinal cords have been severed. The swords were inserted into their hearts postmortem. But Mr. Faulkner died because the knife struck his heart. He was killed quite differently."

"Then why did you not notice this at the crime scene?" The detective asked. "Why was there no sign of hemorrhaging on their necks at the crime scene?"

The doctor answered: "If you look more carefully at the skin of the neck around the holes, you will notice a sort of burn. In fact, the diameter of the holes on the necks was much larger than what you see now. But the type of burn caused the skin to retract and cover the surface of the holes to a great extent. I think some sort of acid substance caused the burns. That is why I failed to notice these holes when I first looked at them."

The detective asked: "What do you think was the instrument used to make these holes?"

But before the doctor could answer, Officer Williams expressed his opinion: "Perhaps they were made by a very sharp double-pronged steel object."

The doctor looked at both and said, "These holes were made by teeth."

"Teeth?"

The doctor said: "Yes, teeth. We noticed something strange in the photographs that we took of the necks of the two victims. When we opened the back of Mrs. Hopkins' neck and removed the shattered bones, the broken tip of an incisor tooth was founded amid the shattered bones. After DNA testing, it became clear that this tooth did not belong to any known animal! Of course, I have another bit of news for you. I had told you that the fingerprinting team has come to a strange conclusion. In fact, the prints that were found on the handles of the two swords do not belong to a human being at all!"

The detective and Officer Williams looked at each other, puzzled.

Chapter 32

When she reached the bottom of the stairs, she had not taken more than a few steps when two men in black suits came toward her. The older one said, "I apologize for troubling you." Then gesturing to the younger man, he said, "Officer Williams! Show the photo to the lady!"

As Elena reached for the photo, the detective continued: "Do you recognize this person? We found your cell phone number in his pocket."

Elena held up the photo and looked at it carefully. Then she said in a surprised tone, "Yes. What has happened to Thomas?"

The man looked straight into Elena's eyes and said: "We found his body last night with a sword pierced through his heart."

Chapter 33

Elena fiddled with her hair and then said: "Why would Thomas write my number on a piece of paper and put it in this pocket? He could have easily stored my number on his cell phone."

But George, who was engulfed in his own thoughts, as though something was distracting him, stared at Elena and said: "What is the meaning of that symbol? That's the same symbol we saw in Mr. Faulkner's safe and in the handwritten manuscript of Nostradamus! This symbol might be the very clue that we're looking for."

"I agree with you," Elena said. "Perhaps Nostradamus used the symbol as a secret code, a code that in some unknown way is related to the recent incidents."

"We have to decipher this secret code!" George responded.

Elena pressed the palms of her hands on the desk, lifting herself onto the desk, and said: "Each of the things that we know is like a small dot; and when we find the correlation between these dots and connect them to one another, we can find the answer. Of course, we need to figure out which dot we have to connect to which dot. Well, we'd better read the quatrains once again."

But before she got off the desk, George pointed to a book on the desk, right beside where Elena was sitting, and then said: "It's exactly like the picture on the cover of the book; we can figure out that the depiction of a bear is hidden among all these stars when we connect the brighter stars together."

When she heard all this, Elena stared at the cover of the book, and a few seconds later jumped off the desk and went to her laptop to look once again at the photographs that Arthur had emailed to her. Suddenly, her face changed and she shouted with excitement: "George! You are a genius! You discovered the secret code of Nostradamus!"

"I have no idea what you're talking about!"

"Just hold on a second, you'll get it," Elena said. She connected her laptop to a small printer and printed two of the photographs. She took out her red fluorescent marker from her desk drawer and connected the brighter stars on the printed pictures with lines. Then she said in her playfully teasing tone, "What do you see now?"

Amazingly, the same strange symbol appeared before George's astounded eyes. "This is extraordinary; it's exactly the same **symbol**!" he said.

Elena went back to her laptop again and said: "Now we have to see whether or not any black hole has been discovered within the area shown in these photographs." She typed the word "NASA," hit "Enter," and then after a search that took about half an hour, she was able to find the answer. The answer was in the affirmative. Elena was right, somewhere beyond the area of the same photographs, NASA had discovered a new black hole. And this was only the beginning of their adventure.

Chapter 34

Two police officers by the names of Jimmy and Emily were patrolling in a police car when suddenly they heard someone yelling, "Help, help..." Jimmy slammed his foot on the brake, stopped the car, and said to his colleague, "Did you hear that, too?"

Emily said, "Yes, someone was calling for help."

They exchanged glances and then both stepped out of the car cautiously and walked in the direction of the voice. Emily listened carefully. She could hear someone panting. She pointed her finger toward a car parked at the side of the street and made sure that Jimmy understood that he should check it out. They were getting closer to the car when suddenly blood gushed out into the air from the other side of the car. They both quickly drew their weapons. The moon shown on Jimmy's shiny metal weapon. They looked at each other, signaled to each other with a nod, and jumped in a sudden move toward the car; but what they saw was unbelievable to them. They were looking at a humanoid creature with blood dripping from its long incisors sitting next to the corpse of a young woman. With his yellow-colored eyes, which seemed to be made of sparks of fire, he looked at the two young police officers. But just as he was about to attack Jimmy, Emily fired a shot at the vampire creature, and the bullet went through his shoulder. The vampire cried out in pain, and then started to run away very fast. He was running so fast that they were unable to chase him on foot. Jimmy and Emily quickly got into their car and drove after him.

They had chased him for two hours, but they had lost his track. The running speed of this vampire had amazed them both, and they were still patrolling the streets, hoping to find some sign of him. Jimmy turned the steering wheel, and as they passed a bend in the street, an orange-colored Ferrari, which had stopped a short distance from them, caught their eyes. No more than a few moments had passed when thick smoke rose into the air from the back tires of the orange car, and a few moments later, the Ferrari took off at tremendous speed down the street. Jimmy looked at Emily and said: "If we were not looking for the vampire, I would show this crazy driver what's what and make sure that she never again mistakes the streets for a racetrack."

Chapter 35

Her golden hair was dancing in the breeze; and as both of them sat next to each other on the flat stone ledge of the window less than half a meter wide, with their legs dangling down seven meters from the ground watching the sunset, swinging her legs in the air, Elena said: "I will travel to that black hole. I must avenge the blood of the Hopkins family and find the rest of the missing quatrains. The rest of the prophecies might help me learn about other unpleasant incidents that are supposed to occur in the future, in order to be able to prevent the destruction of Planet Earth. But what do you want to do, George? From now on, we have even more difficult work and greater dangers ahead. Will you be my fellow traveler, or would you rather stay right here?"

Filled with emotion, George stared into Elena's eyes. It was a very romantic moment. With heartfelt sentiment, he said: "I will never leave you alone. No matter how dangerous this is going to be, it is not important to me. If I am going to be killed, I want to die beside you. I will come with you; but I still don't know how you plan to travel to a black hole in space."

Elena looked at him compassionately, smiled, and said, "We must continue the path of my father!"

"I don't understand what you mean."

Elena held his hand and said: "Come with me! I want to show you something."

They both turned around, toward Elena's room, grabbed the window frame, and slowly jumped to the floor of the room. Still holding George's hand, Elena started walking to the room across from her office on the left side of the staircase, turned the shiny metal door handle with her right hand, and opened the door. The room was dark; and part of the light of the chandeliers hanging from the ceiling of the great room caused the shadows of George and Elena to stretch so far on the lit rectangle of the wooden floor of the room that the extensions of the shadows of their heads reflected on the wall of the room in front of them. Elena turned the light on and a very luxurious, beautiful room became visible. The floor, the bookshelves, and a few sofas and chairs, and even the picture frame on the wall with the photograph of a middle-aged man in an astronaut's suit were all made of oak.

George asked: "Did you want to show me your father's room?"

Without answering, Elena went directly to the bookshelves that covered the entire left wall from the floor to the ceiling, pushed a few books aside, and pressed a small golden button that was hidden behind the books. The bookshelf shook lightly; one part of the bookshelf moved to the right and another to the left, revealing in the middle a secret pathway. Elena gestured to George with her hand and said: "Hurry up, come with me! We're still two light switches away from the main surprise."

They both walked along the dark hallway. After a few steps, Elena pressed a light switch. Now George could clearly see the elevator a few steps away from them. They got into the elevator and began to descend, as though they were moving toward the center of the earth. George continued to prepare himself for the surprise that Elena had promised. The elevator went down about sixty meters and then stopped quietly.

"Alright, we have arrived," Elena said. The sound of their footsteps on the hard floor under their feet could be heard until they found themselves before a large metal door. Using the buttons next to the metal door, Elena entered some numbers for the secret code. A few minutes later, the gigantic door began to move. They stepped into pitch darkness. George had no clue where they were until Elena put her finger on the light switch, the same light switch that she had promised, and 120 very powerful spotlights mounted in the sixty-meter high ceiling lit up a very large area somewhat like a huge underground hall. On the wall at the end of the hall was a very large round hole, the bottom of which could not be seen. It looked like a hole dug by an extremely large mole, the diameter of the body of which would have been twenty-five meters. A gigantic cylinder-shaped machine, the diameter of which was about the same as the hole in the wall, was about 100 meters away from George, and several large metal doors could be seen in the concrete walls of the hall. But George was staring at something else. Looking up, he was staring not at the ceiling but at a very large orange-colored fuel tank, about fifty meters high. In addition, two other fuel tanks, which looked like white missiles, were placed on both sides of the orange fuel tank.

Still staring, George said, "Oh my God, what is this?"

Elena answered: "About a year ago, my father found out that he had cancer. He did not want to die in bed. He was always an adventurer, and now that he realized his death was near, he wanted to experience the greatest adventure of his life and do something that no other human being would have either the ability or the courage to do. He had decided to travel to a black hole, and he was determined to do this with his old friend, the Space Shuttle *Discovery*. He had many memories of the Space Shuttle *Discovery*, and he did not want his lovely shuttle to die in a museum, and he himself in a bed. He wanted to face death in the shuttle that he was so fond of while experiencing the greatest adventure in history. So, he decided to implement his plan. He discussed the plan with a group of his friends that he trusted in the Space Agency, and a number of them agreed to carry out his last wish before he died. Of course, my father would pay the entire cost of this project; and he decided to spend even more to use specialists from other countries for this project. Using a TBM, a tunnel boring machine, and at great expense in terms of both time and money, they built this underground base and prepared all the necessary equipment to start the operations of the shuttle flight control center. After the work was completed on building a liquid fuel storage tank and two solid fuel rockets, the time had come to implement the most critical part of the plan, in other words, stealing the Space Shuttle *Discovery* from the National Air and Space Museum in Washington, DC. If they were to succeed in stealing the shuttle from the museum, then they would have to add, once again, very important parts that had been removed in order to transfer the shuttle to the museum; and after a series of modifications to the space shuttle, the conditions were prepared for flight. My father had a plan for stealing the shuttle. With the TBM that they had used to build this place, he intended to dig an underground tunnel all the way to the Smithsonian Air and Space Museum in Washington and overnight steal the shuttle and bring it here. The digging operations began, but before the tunnel could reach the Air and Space Museum in Washington, my father died of cancer. Everything was left unfinished; and this place was forgotten. But I think that now is the time for me to continue my father's path."

"But how?" George said. "Even if we successfully implement all of your father's plan, how can we go on this space travel, since we are not astronauts?

Pausing for a moment, Elena said: "You'll find out soon. For now, let's take a look together at this place." They first went toward the gigantic cylinder-shaped machine. Elena patted the body of the machine and in her usual playful tone said: "The hole in the wall is the work of this little mouse. This is the TBM I was talking about. In fact, it's the largest drill in the world."

George looked at the machine and said: "The largest drill in the world! It is indeed a worthy title." In fact, this was the largest TBM built in the world.

A few minutes later, Elena showed George a large metal door on which the word "Exit" appeared in red letters. There was a private side road behind the door, which led to the ground level at about a 26-degree angle and connected to a wider road. Elena explained to George that all the equipment had been transferred to this place through this route. She then took George's hand, and together they walked toward another metal door. The door opened and the white lights on the ceiling lit up the hall. It was a relatively large hall, the ceiling of which was about four meters from the ground. Three gigantic monitors were installed on the black wall at the end of the hall, and nineteen arched rows contained the computer systems, each row including three or four PC-size monitors. The rows, equidistant from each other, faced the wall at the end of the room.

In fact, they were arranged in such a way that dozens of people could be working in this room and would be able to view the three gigantic monitors clearly.

"What is this place supposed to be?" George questioned.

"Well, this is the space shuttle flight control room."

"How did your father plan to bring together all these specialists for the shuttle flight control?"

"With $300 million, problems can be solved," Elena explained, "and you can bring in specialists from throughout the world; precisely what I will do in a few days. In addition to the specialists in the United States, we can bring in a number of specialists from Russia or China. Well, we have nothing else to do here. Now, I would like to show you another hall where we have a lot to do tomorrow morning."

Another metal door opened. Yellow lights lit up the hall. The instruments and equipment in that room caught George's attention: a small glass chamber the dimensions of which could only accommodate one person; a bulletproof glass globe in which openings had been made to place wrists and ankles and that was placed in a cube-shaped apparatus and could spin in various directions, and its speed and turning direction were regulated by a computer system; a jet engine placed vertically in the ground in such a way that its propellers were facing the ceiling and upon which a metal netting was installed; and so on. In addition to the equipment in the room, a relatively small but very deep pool was in the corner of the hall, about 30 meters deep. While George was looking around bewildered, Elena began explaining about the equipment, starting with the glass chamber: "This is a vacuum chamber. Using this, you can build up your body's resistance under low-pressure conditions. This chamber empties the air inside it to the point that the air pressure reaches zero. Of course, under such conditions, a person is certain to die." She then moved toward the globe-shaped object inside the cube-shaped apparatus. Elena made the necessary adjustments using the keyboard on the apparatus, and then she pressed a green button. The globe-shaped object began to revolve. Elena said: "This device can increase your resistance to the spinning and turning movements that would likely happen under conditions of weightlessness." Then she went to the jet engine installed in the ground and on the top of which, at ground level, metal netting was placed. Upon starting the jet engine, a very strong airflow began to blow upward toward the ceiling. The airflow resulting from the turning of the engine's propellers was so strong that it would neutralize the weight of any person standing on the metal netting and would suspend him in the air. Elena put on a bat-like costume and jumped on the netting. While suspended in the air, she said: "This jet engine helps you experience weightlessness, in other words, the condition that you will encounter in the space shuttle. Now, please turn off the engine." Elena's feet returned to the ground.

George glanced at the corner of the room and said: "It's great that we have a pool. Whenever we get tired, we can splash around a little."

"A thirty-meter deep pool is not a good place for splashing around."

"Do you mean this pool is thirty meters deep?" George asked as they walked in the direction of the pool.

Elena dropped a heavy weight tied to the end of a gaged rope into the pool and told George, "Read the number on the rope."

"Precisely thirty meters! But why did they build this pool so deep?"

"Being placed deep in water is one sort of exercise for your body to be able to endure greater pressure. Well, in addition to this training, from tomorrow, you will also have to learn how to pilot the shuttle."

George asked, "Who is going to train us to be pilots?"

"No one else is going to train us," Elena said. "I will train you to become a pilot."

"Very funny! Are you going to tell me that you're also a shuttle pilot?"

"Well, to tell you the truth," Elena explained, "I was not a regular soldier in the military. I was a jetfighter pilot in the military. When I resigned from the military, before I went to Japan, on the suggestion of my father, I passed space shuttle pilot training courses; and of course, I have the experience of participating in one space mission."

George said: "That's really great! Since you are a pilot yourself, there's no need to train me. You can fly the shuttle yourself!"

Elena said: "A space shuttle requires at least two pilots. So, you need to also be trained as a pilot."

George thought about it for moment, and then said: "Well, how about Charlie for this job? At least he knows how to fly a helicopter. I'm sure he would learn how to fly the shuttle much faster than I would."

"How do you expect me to ask Charlie to accompany us to a black hole in space?" Elena queried. "Traveling to a black hole in space is traveling to a completely unknown place; it is a matter of life and death. He has no reason to risk his life to accompany us on this trip. George, you are the only one who can do this!"

"But this is a very difficult thing to do, and we don't have much time," George said.

Elena held George's left arm, and staring into his eyes, she said quietly: "You can do this; I have faith in you."

George dropped his head in submission and said: "OK. I hope I'll be able to do it."

Elena said, "I'm sure you will."

Chapter 36

He was sitting at his rectangular desk, sipping his coffee and immersed in his thoughts, when suddenly the sound of shoes on the stone floor interrupted his thoughts. Officer Williams, accompanied by a tall man, was walking toward the detective. Officer Williams stopped and said: "Sir, this is Commissioner Rogers, from Interpol."

The detective stood up and, shaking the Commissioner's hand, said: "Pleased to meet you, Commissioner. What can I do for you?" Then pointing to a black chair, he said, "Please, have a seat!"

Holding a brown leather briefcase tightly in his hand, Commissioner Rogers looked around the room. Glancing at the commendations on the wall, he sat down and immediately said, "Detective, I need to speak with you in private."

The detective looked at Officer Williams and said: "Officer Williams, you can go back your own work." He left the room, shutting the door behind him.

The Commissioner took a deep breath and said: "I would like to speak to you about an important matter. Have you heard the news about the death of the special aid to the Pope?"

"Yes," The detective said. "I assume you're talking about the person who had a heart attack and died in the archives of the Vatican."

"He did not die," said the Commissioner; "he was murdered."

Detective Anderson asked: "Then, why didn't the police announce the news of the murder? Why did say that he died of a heart attack?"

"On the request of the Vatican," he said. "In fact, the Vatican does not want the news of the killing of the aid to the Pope to become public."

"This is impossible. You know yourself that Interpol has its own protocols and does not take orders from the Vatican."

Commissioner Rogers remained silent for a few moments, and then sighing, he put his hand in the pocket of his jacket, took out a letter and handed it to the detective. At the bottom of the letter was the special seal of the Vatican. The Commissioner took a deep breath and then said: "To tell you the truth, I'm not an agent of Interpol. In fact, I'm a private detective, and I have been assigned by the Vatican to secretly find the murderer."

Surprised, Detective Anderson asked: "Why did the Vatican not inform the police, and rather than informing the police, it is asking a private detective to secretly investigate the murder?"

"Mr. Hopkins was a professor of genetics," Detective Rogers explained. "When the Pope announced that human cloning is a cardinal sin and must be prevented, Professor Hopkins was the only person who openly opposed the Pope, and even wrote him a letter. Considering that the murder took place in the archives of the Vatican, if this news had become public, most likely many of the reporters and journalists who look for controversial subjects would have tried to link this murder to the murder of Mr. Hopkins, to get the Vatican involved in the story and to blame the Vatican for these murders."

Detective Anderson asked: "But what does the murder of Mr. Hopkins have to do with the murder of the special aid to the Pope?"

He replied: "Because they found the body in the archives of the Vatican with a sword penetrating his heart."

Detective Anderson looked surprised and said: "Does this mean that you think the murderer is the same person who killed Mr. and Mrs. Hopkins? Then, this is the reason why you have come to see me."

"Yes, Detective. It is quite likely," Rogers said. "The findings of the coroner indicate that the victim did not die from the stab wound; rather, he was killed before that. I would like to ask you if the vertebrae in the necks of Mr. and Mrs. Hawkins were broken?"

The detective said: "Yes, in fact, on the necks of each of the bodies are two holes, and before the swords pierced their hearts, the bones of the vertebrae on the necks had been broken."

Rogers said: "I am now certain that the murders of Mr. and Mrs. Hopkins are also the work of the vampires."

The detective repeated with curiosity: "Vampires! What are you talking about?"

Detective Rogers opened his brown leather briefcase, took out a sheet of paper, handed it to Detective Anderson, and said: "This is a copy of a document that was stolen from the archives of the Vatican at the time of the murder. I think that the special aid to the Pope was killed in the archives because of this document, since this is the only document in the archives that was stolen at the same time as this murder."

Detective Anderson glanced at the sheet of paper and said in a surprised tone: "I can't read the writing. What language is it?"

Detective Rogers explained: "It's in German. In fact, this is the letter that Beethoven wrote to the Pope.

In this letter, Beethoven tells the Pope that he had witnessed a strange incident, an incident that if he were to tell other people, they would think he had gone mad. He tells the Pope that he had seen a demonic creature, a creature that uses its long incisors to feed on human blood, a creature whose eyes are made of sparks of fire. In his letter, Beethoven writes that such creatures might be agents of Satan, and that perhaps Armageddon has come and Satan has mobilized an army of demonic creatures for a great battle, and for this reason, the only person who can make the people aware and tell them..."

Detective Anderson asked: "Detective Rogers, why don't you finish what you were saying? Tell them what?"

"Because Beethoven's letter is not complete," he explained. "The final words are 'tell them,' and Beethoven does not finish. Despite the fact that this sheet of paper was copied from the original and was given to the decoding team at the Vatican for two years, the shading that resulted from the printer's ink on the sheet of paper makes it quite clear that the original letter had been crushed intentionally. Considering that the letter is unfinished, and that this letter was made available to the Vatican years after the death of Beethoven, I think that while Beethoven was writing this letter, he changed his mind. Well, now you know why I said that the murderer must be a vampire!"

The detective thought for a second or two and then said: "Why was this letter given to the decoding team for two years?"

Rogers said: "In fact, the decoding team at the Vatican did not work on the text of this letter, but it worked on decoding the musical notes that Beethoven had written on the back of the letter. They are some notes that seem to be part of a melody, but no such melody exists in any of the pieces of music written by Beethoven. The strange point is that instead of using the sol key to start writing his notes, Beethoven used a strange, odd symbol. Of course, the first part of this symbol greatly resembles the sol key; but when the decoding team replaced this symbol with the sol key, they realized that this melody would become off key, and to place these notes side by side would be completely discordant. They even replaced this symbol with the fa key; but it was of no use, and again the melody was off key, and the notes placed next to each other were completely discordant. But how is it possible for the greatest composer in the world to write an off-key and completely discordant melody?"

Upon hearing these words, the expression on Detective Anderson's face completely changed. Immediately, he looked at the back of the sheet of paper on which he could now see the same strange symbol next to the notes written by Beethoven that he had seen

at the bottom of Professor Faulkner's safe. Astounded,
he mumbled, **"The Beethoven code!"**

Chapter 37

She listened as the telephone rang twice, then Elena said: "Hello, Mr. Hoffman, this is Elena..." She had contacted other persons in the same way. She was sitting in her office, and before going into the underground hall to train George as an astronaut, she had contacted about fifteen other people. In fact, Elena was carrying out the preparations for the project, the project of stealing the space shuttle and traveling to the black hole. For this reason, she had telephone conversations with a number of her father's old friends, as well as her own friends who had previously been her colleagues at the Space Agency. Ten of the sixteen contacts had responded positively and agreed to work with Elena. She took a deep breath and prepared herself to go to the underground hall.

Chapter 38

[One month before the skulls were stolen]

He was overwhelmed with excitement, as though he had made a discovery. He knocked on the door of the office twice, and without waiting for permission, entered the office and hastily closed the door behind him. Mrs. Hopkins, who was sitting at her desk, looked at him over the rim of her glasses and asked: "Mr. Franklin! Did you want to see me?"

With excitement in his voice, he responded: "Yes, Professor. I have finally chosen the topic for my dissertation."

"What is the topic that you have chosen?"

"It is about Shakespeare. In fact, I should say that it is about Shakespeare's curse."

Removing her glasses, Mrs. Hopkins said in a surprised tone: "Shakespeare! But I think that this topic is more suitable for a doctoral dissertation in literature than in history! Could you explain further?"

Hurriedly, Mr. Franklin opened his briefcase, took out a stack of old papers, and walking with them to Mrs. Hopkins' desk, said: "I found this play in the archives of the university library. It is a play by Shakespeare. I am certain that it is in his own handwriting."

Mrs. Hopkins took the play with curiosity and glanced at it.

Mr. Franklin continued: "If you look carefully, on the upper left-hand corner of the second page, you can see a part of a poem. It is very faint, but it is still legible. I spoke to a literature professor who said that this poem does not exist among Shakespeare's poetry and that this was the first time that he had seen this piece of poetry. Despite the fact that it is an incomplete poem, in my opinion, it resembles some sort of prophecy. I think that there has to be a connection between this piece of poetry and the poem that Shakespeare composed for his gravestone, the one known as Shakespeare's curse, the poem that reads:

GOOD FREND FOR JESUS SAKE FOREBEARE

TO DIGG THE DUST ENCLOASED HEARE

BLESTE BE YE MAN THAT SPARES THES STONES

AND CURST BE HE THAT MOVES MY BONES

"It is as though some mystery is hidden in both poems, which he wanted to reveal to us. Perhaps the strange symbol at the side of the poem can solve this puzzle. I need your help to uncover the meaning of this symbol."

Mrs. Hopkins, however, continued to stare at that **symbol** without uttering a word.

Chapter 39

In a loud voice while pressing his eyes closed, George shouted, "Stop it!"

Elena pushed the red button on the keypad. The spinning movement of the glass globe-shaped chamber stopped. George came out of it staggering, sat on the ground, sank his head into a plastic bucket, and vomited. Walking toward him with a white handkerchief, Elena said: "You only have fifteen minutes to rest. After that, your pilot training class begins." George wiped his mouth with the handkerchief and got up off the ground.

A tremendously loud roaring sound was heard, and the drills of the gigantic digging machine began to turn. In addition to the spinning movement, this machine was driven forward with great pressure jacks, and the result of these two movements was the digging of the earth in the heart of the tunnel. The earth was transferred through the control openings installed at the tip of the digging drills to a conveyor belt more than fifty meters long alongside the machine, and after a series of processes, the earth was transported outside the underground hall by trucks. Elena was standing next to George, and watching the operations, she explained to him about the machine. An engineer wearing a yellow safety helmet raised his voice and said: "Turn off the machines. We will continue the work in two hours."

Finally, the roaring sound of the machine stopped. George and Elena were inside the tunnel next to the long conveyor belt. George pointed to one of the hundreds of thick pipes sticking out of the wall of the tunnel, and asked with curiosity, "What are these pipes for?"

Elena explained: "These pipes play the most important role in this project. They are connected to very large reservoirs, each of which has the capacity for about 40,000 cubic meters of concrete. After we succeed in stealing the space shuttle and we transfer it here through this tunnel, the work of the pipes will begin. They will pump hundreds of thousands of cubic meters of concrete into the tunnel at very high speed. By doing so, the route to the tunnel will be sealed, and no one will be able to come after us." She then looked at her watch and said: "Well, resting time is over. I would like to teach you some things today that are very important. You must fully concentrate. We'd better get going right away."

Pallor and fatigue were evident on George's face, the skin of which was very swollen. He was not able to stand on his legs any longer. Elena pressed the button quickly, and when the door to the glass chamber opened, she hurriedly removed the special oxygen helmet that was on George's head and pulled him out of the vacuum chamber. It took a few minutes for George to completely recover. Elena said: "Compared to a month ago, you have made great progress. You were able to endure the conditions inside the chamber." Then, without waiting to hear any response from George, she picked up a black marker, ready to start her teaching with the white board. They had to make maximum use of the time they had, and every minute was priceless to them.

Chapter 40

The night seemed very quiet, and the building of the Smithsonian museum shown under the moonlight. Inside the museum, the Space Shuttle *Discovery* was resting peacefully, when suddenly the sharp, powerful drills of the digging machine made a hole through the floor of the museum hall, and a roaring sound filled the hall for a few seconds. A few minutes later, George and Elena approached the shuttle with flashlights in their hands. The circular light of the flashlight in George's hand shone on one of the wings of the shuttle, and the word "Discovery" appeared before their eyes. They examined the shuttle carefully to find suitable places to fasten the steel cables. After carefully fastening three steel cables to the shuttle, Elena signaled with her finger to a driver of a large bulldozer to start moving. They had rapidly removed the TBM from the tunnel, and now, a gigantic bulldozer was pulling the *Discovery* behind it. After the shuttle was successfully transferred to the underground hall, hundreds of thick pipes that were in the walls of the tunnel began to pump concrete into the tunnel at tremendous speed; and a few hours later, there was no sign of the tunnel, which was replaced with concrete blocks several kilometers long. Now the operations for stealing the Space Shuttle *Discovery* had been completed successfully.

Chapter 41

A bare hand wiped the steam on the bathroom mirror, and George's image appeared in the mirror. He was staring at the burn on his left arm that looked like a brand. He was about to touch it with his right hand when he suddenly heard Elena's voice from behind the bathroom door: "George! We don't have much time before the launch. Hurry up a little!"

Now, about two months had passed since the Space Shuttle *Discovery* was stolen. After going through the necessary training and very difficult exercises, George had now become a shuttle pilot. In addition, the shuttle specialists had succeeded in the course of these two months in preparing the engines and other parts that had been removed from it when the Space Shuttle *Discovery* had been transferred to the museum, and had installed them on the shuttle. All of this had cost Elena about $400 million. George picked up his towel and dried himself. Elena looked at her swords, picked them up along with her backpack, and walked toward the secret door in her father's room to board the shuttle. There was a commotion in the space shuttle flight control room. Specialists from various countries were there, sitting behind the computers. Some images appeared on the three gigantic monitors. The solid fuel and liquid fuel storage tanks had been filled, and Elena was proudly looking at the space shuttle, which was placed on the launch platform in the underground hall, with tears running down from the corners of her eyes. Perhaps she wished her father were alive and that he would accompany them on this trip. Now, Elena was fulfilling her father's dream. She was still staring at the shuttle when she felt a heavy hand on her shoulder. It was George.

"I'm ready. Don't you want to board the shuttle?"

Trying to conceal the tears on her face, Elena said with a smile, "Oh, you're right. It's time to go."

After they boarded the space shuttle, the large automatic doors that had been installed at the height of sixty meters inside the ceiling of the hall moved aside slowly. The launch platform on which the shuttle was placed moved upward with the help of gigantic hydraulic jacks, finally stopping after having traveled a distance of sixty meters and reaching ground level. Now the launch platform and the space shuttle were in the green courtyard of Elena's house.

Peter was standing on one of the terraces of the building, slowly wiping his tears with a white handkerchief. Life without the Mistress would be meaningless for Peter; but he was unable to change the Mistress's mind about going on this trip. It was already too late, because the countdown for the shuttle launch had begun: 10, 9, 8, 7, 6, 5, 4, 3, 2, 1. A great deal of thick white smoke exited from the end of the space shuttle, and the shuttle rose into the sky.

Minutes were passing rapidly. Elena and George were sitting in their individual seats. The shuttle had traveled a long distance away from earth. George was nurturing certain ideas in his mind. He knew well that they would be entering the black hole some minutes later, and that the black hole would suck them in. It was unclear what calamity would befall them upon entering the black hole or what awaited them. Both of them might die, and this could be the last time he saw Elena. George's heart was beating rapidly. Before anything happened, he wanted to tell Elena what he felt in his heart. In these past few months, both of them had been so busy that George had not had the opportunity at all to be able to tell Elena what he held in his heart. These remaining minutes were the last chance that George had, and he did not want to lose this chance. So, despite the fact that his heart was beating very fast and he was also breathing very fast, he took two deep breaths. Elena, who had noticed the change in George, glanced at him. George's sparkling familiar eyes were twinkling before Elena like two small candles at the bottom of a well. Now Elena was also feeling a change. Obviously, she could see the love that was evident in George's eyes when she looked into them, the same love that was also visible in Elena's eyes. Hence, before George said anything, Elena took the first step and, looking into George's eyes, slowly she brought her lips close to

George's. George, who could feel the heat from Elena's face, involuntarily brought his face closer to Elena's. As George was merely a few centimeters away from kissing Elena's lips, suddenly a loud siren sounded, signaling they were getting closer to the black hole; it was a sensor installed in the shuttle that measured the intensity of the magnetic field and could specify the proximity of the shuttle to the black hole. They were a short distance from the black hole. Elena jumped up and said: "Oh, my God! We're close to the black hole, and I have not removed it yet."

George, who had become really confused, asked, "What are you talking about?"

Anxiously, Elena said: "You stay where you are; I'll be right back." She then got up, and while suspended in the air, she moved toward an opening to another part of the shuttle. George obeyed Elena, and despite the fact that he was most worried, he did not leave his seat. Time continued to pass. About three minutes had passed since Elena left, and there was no sign of her. George, who could no longer endure it and was most concerned and worried, stood up and moved toward the same opening. But after passing through the opening, he was faced with a horrible scene. Elena's body was suspended in the air with one of her swords pierced deeply into her heart. Elena's eyes were open, staring at the ceiling, and her clothes were soaked in blood. Suddenly, everything was engulfed in absolute darkness, and George a felt great pressure on his body. He had now entered the black hole.

End of volume one